Negotiating Skills

LAUREL CREMANT

WINGED MOON
PUBLISHING

Negotiating Skills
Copyright © 2016 by Laurel Cremant

ISBN: 978-09916357-3-3

Cover Art by Taria Reed Digital Artist
Print First Edition

Winged Moon Publishing, LLC
Hollywood, Florida

This is a work of fiction. Names, characters, places, and incidents either are the product of the author's imagination or are used fictitiously, and any resemblance to actual persons living or dead, business establishments, events or locales, is entirely confidential.

Witnessing a private act leads to some interesting negotiations...

Software programmer Veronica James is struggling to make her new business a success. After finally landing a major account, she's at risk of losing it all when she catches her new client Victor Rossi in a very compromising position. In an effort to regain the upper hand, Rossi insists on some sexy and compromising concessions from her that have Veronica reconsidering her hard fast rule of not mixing business with pleasure.

To my amazingly loving and supportive husband who has always pushed me to do what I love and never let me settle when it comes to my dreams.

A heartfelt thanks also goes out to all of my family and friends who were still willing to speak to me even after days, weeks, and months of me being sequestered away with only my laptop unplugged from the net and a cell phone switched definitively off.

CHAPTER | ONE

*I*t *all came down to odds.*

Veronica sat in the plush waiting room of Niles Enterprises. One good contract to tilt the odds in her favor and she'd be set. All she needed was one good break.

"Just one big client," she muttered to herself. Hopefully, the one she waited to meet.

Glancing down, she checked her watch for what felt like the thousandth time. She had been waiting for almost thirty minutes—and the longer the delay, the more tightly wound she became.

The delay to meet with Victor Rossi, the owner and CEO of Niles Enterprises, had her stomach cramping in nervousness. Niles Enterprises specialized in property management. The business owned a slew of properties throughout Florida and the East coast and, as of two weeks ago, was in need of a software programmer.

According to her sources, about a year ago, the company hired a team of developers to build a software application suite meant to help the company's individual properties manage their billing and accounts. The application was nicknamed CLEO, but unfortunately, the lead developer and software architect recently quit and took all of the code with him.

The company was desperately in need of a new lead developer to finish the project, and she was hoping to fill that spot—if only temporarily.

"He'll only be a few more minutes."

Veronica glanced up at the sound of the smooth, modulated voice. The woman who had introduced herself as Rossi's assistant strolled into the room from an adjacent doorway, which Veronica assumed led to Rossi's office.

"He had a conference call that ran a little over," the cool blonde said as she took a seat behind her desk and began typing on her computer with easy efficiency.

"No problem." Veronica smiled briefly at the woman and tried not to let her impatience and nervousness show.

Don't panic. You can do this.

She took in a few calming breaths. Yes, this job would be the break she needed and she would get it. She thought back to the events of the last two years and felt a surge of confidence flow through her body. She was proud of her herself and her business and she was damn good at what she did. She had moved down to Miami two years ago after deciding to finally leave her position as junior developer at a big software firm in New York. After years of working extra hours and taking on additional assignments, she had grown tired of waiting for the opportunity to manage her own projects. Unfortunately, the programming world was still very much male-dominated, and despite being one of her firm's best programmers, she was passed up several times for promotion.

Starting her own company was one of the best decisions she ever made. The move to Miami had been a fresh start, a new city where she could break away and start her own custom software application development firm.

Thankfully, the start-up costs for programming were relatively low. All she needed were her computer and a desk to get started. After a few months, she had picked up a few good clients and, within a year, had managed to garner a steady amount of work.

But not enough to get her to the next level.

She needed to land an account big enough to give her enough wiggle room financially to hire on a junior developer. Once she had additional help, she could start pursuing larger accounts. Unfortunately, reaching the next level still took getting that one big break.

Her hopes hinged on convincing Victor Rossi that he needed a dedicated software firm—specifically hers— and not a new lead developer to handle the project.

She'd worked on her pitch from the moment she heard news about the opening at Niles. She knew her numbers were solid, and that she could handle the job. The trick was convincing Rossi.

"I'm ready now, Marie."

The disembodied voice startled Veronica out of her thoughts. She struggled not to leap from her chair and sprint straight to the adjacent office door and babble her proposal to Rossi in an excited jumble.

Instead, she looked up calmly to see his assistant rise from her desk and open the adjacent office door before signaling for her to enter.

"He'll see you now."

"Thank you." Veronica rose from her chair and walked towards the door.

She paused briefly at the threshold and took another fortifying breath. *Time for your "A" game*, she told herself as she smiled widely and entered the office.

CHAPTER | TWO

Victor was surprised to see his assistant usher a young woman into his office. According to his planner, he was scheduled to interview a software programmer named Ronnie who could hopefully take on the task of completing an application suite for the company.

His conference call had run late, and he had already kept the man waiting. The company needed someone on board as soon as possible and wanted to get the required interview over with.

Taking a quick appraisal of the young woman walking in, he had to admit she was a beautiful distraction. She had smooth caramel skin and features that, alone, would be considered just pretty. But coupled with her high cheekbones and pouty mouth, they were visually striking and deserved more than a second look.

As she approached his desk, Victor couldn't help but wonder if the curves beneath her boxy pant suit were as rounded as her lush lips. His appraisal stopped at her feet and he fought back a surprised lift of his brow.

The woman wore the boxiest suit he'd seen since the 1980's, but had on the sexiest pair of black pumps.

"Thank you for agreeing to meet with me, Mr. Rossi. I really appreciate your time." She smiled at him and put out her hand.

He frowned slightly as he took her proffered hand, wondering if Marie had made a mistake with his schedule.

"My pleasure, Ms....?"

"James, Veronica James," she replied quickly, an impish smile quirking her lips. "Ronnie is short for Veronica," she continued at his confused look. "I got the nickname early in my career and it just kind of stuck professionally."

A slight, upward shrug of her shoulders accompanied the statement.

For the first time, he noticed a small portfolio case clutched in her hand. He was surprised that he'd missed the telling piece of evidence when she first walked in.

"Ah. Yes, then please have a seat." He gestured towards one of the custom acrylic chairs facing his desk.

He watched as she sat down, and noticed the quick look of surprise cross her face as she settled into the chair. He was used to the look from first-time visitors to his office. The chairs were a clear acrylic, buffed to look like glass. Most people assumed they would be hard and uncomfortable, but although he was a big fan of minimalist design, he was an even bigger fan of comfort. He had chosen the chairs himself, appreciating their clear, sleek look, and liking their comfortable design.

"Again, thank you for agreeing to meet with me on such short notice," she said, settling into her seat.

"Of course, I'm hoping to fill this position as soon as possible." He glanced down at the resume on his desk. "So, tell me about yourself."

"Well, first of all, I have to tell you I'm not here to interview to be your new lead developer," Veronica said in an apologetic tone.

"Excuse me?" Victor quirked an eyebrow.

"I'm not here to interview to be your lead developer," she repeated as she flipped open her portfolio case and withdrew a presentation folio. "I don't think what you need is a new lead developer."

She flopped open the folder and placed it in on the desk in front of him.

"I've got an entire project time line that would disagree with you, Ms. James. I don't have time to waste on useless meetings."

He felt his lips turn down in a frown and didn't bother to hide his irritation. He was working against a deadline and didn't appreciate anyone wasting his time. *No matter how attractive the distraction is*, he thought as he slid his gaze over her face.

"I don't plan on wasting anyone's time," she insisted. "I propose that you outsource the entire project. I've outlined the details in this report."

She leaned forward and tapped her finger on the report open in front of him. A report he had yet to glance at since she placed it on his desk.

Victor merely shook his head at her, still not looking at the papers.

"I'm a firm believer in keeping my business local. I see no point in sending work outside of the states when there are perfectly capable workers right here," he said as he pushed the documents back towards her.

"I'm not talking about outsourcing to another country. I'm talking about outsourcing the project to outside of Niles Enterprises," she said, pushing the report back to him. "Right now, you're suffering from not having a dedicated application development department. You hired a developer with no oversight, and no one on your management team is able to decipher his jargon and double speak. I'm proposing a different approach," she stated calmly but firmly, leaning back in her chair.

Victor leaned back in his executive seat and stared at the woman in front of him. She seemed to be convinced of her words. The question was whether she had the talent to follow through.

Thinking about how he'd been blindsided when Brian, his old lead developer, jumped ship and took a year's worth of work with him, he gave a mental shrug and decided to at least hear the woman out.

"What do you have in mind?" he asked finally.

He watched her release a slow, pent-up breath, and couldn't hold back a grin. The woman had grit and he was interested in learning what she thought she had to offer his company.

He listened as she launched into a speech that was obviously well-rehearsed.

"I propose that you contract with an established developer to handle the project. A contract will be worked up guaranteeing full rights to the application to Niles Enterprises."

She threw out a quick smile before she continued. "Specifically, with my company."

"And why would I want to use you?" Victor asked, more than slightly amused by her show of confidence. "Why shouldn't I just go with a more established company?"

"Because you wouldn't get top priority there," she said, leaning forward in her seat again. "I can offer you complete exclusivity. You would be guaranteed that all billable hours would be dedicated to only you."

Victor quirked an eyebrow at her bold statement. He wondered if she realized how tantalizing her statement sounded, and just how easily her meaning could be misconstrued. Although, he had to admit she had a point.

At the beginning stages of CLEO, he had considered going to an outside company, when the idea of developing an application for the company had first arisen. However, after interviewing some software companies, he wasn't satisfied that his project would receive the appropriate amount of attention.

Finally looking down at the proposal on his desk, he began flipping through the pages. After a few minutes of reading in silence, he had to admit the woman had done her research. He actually began to hope that the project might be salvaged, after all. After a few more minutes of review, he glanced up at her and held her direct gaze.

"You have my attention, Ms. James," he said before glancing down at his watch. "You have twenty minutes to convince me that you're worth the risk."

He leaned back in his seat and folded his hands across his stomach.

Veronica left Victor Rossi's office, a wide smile stretching across her face as she made her way out of the building and back to her car. Although Rossi had originally given her only twenty minutes for her pitch, their meeting had extended to over an hour. Once she began her presentation, time had flown by as they discussed the pros and cons of her proposal.

To her surprise, he had asked well-informed

questions, leading her to believe he had at least some background familiarity with software programming. His knowledge of code wasn't the only thing that had taken her aback. When she first walked into the office, his appearance had surprised her.

She had expected a much older man. Instead, Victor Rossi didn't look to be any older than thirty-five, maybe forty at the most.

He had dark, almost black, hair, a trim goatee, and green eyes that stood out dramatically against his pale skin. His strong, Roman features spoke of a Mediterranean, or perhaps, Middle Eastern heritage.

When he first stood to greet her, she couldn't help but notice how his suit jacket pulled tautly against the solid muscles of his chest. He wasn't overly tall, but at about six feet in height, he easily towered over her five-foot-three frame.

Veronica was woman enough to admit she found him attractive, but smart enough to push that attraction aside and ignore the pull. Her priority was to wow him and win his business, not jump into his pants.

At his twenty-minute declaration, she'd

launched into her presentation. He had let her speak virtually uninterrupted for those first twenty minutes. But once she finished her presentation, he'd voiced a series of pointed questions.

At first, she'd feared he was merely building a case to deny her proposal. However, she soon realized he was actually negotiating with her, determining the best way to implement her ideas into the framework of his project.

"You'll still have to pass a background check," he said.

"Not a problem."

"And I expect work to begin immediately."

"If you can get me access to the right files today, and a meeting with the remaining team, I can get started this afternoon," she said, a smile stretching across face.

"I expect you to be available for all meetings and all questions."

"Consider me already on speed dial. I *did* guarantee complete exclusivity." Her smile grew.

"Well, then I guess we have a deal, Ms. James," he said as he pushed his chair back and stood, reaching his hand out to shake hers.

Veronica had stared at his outstretched hand for a few seconds. Despite spending the last hour discussing and defending her proposal and beginning to hope that Rossi would give her a chance, she was still slightly shocked when he'd agreed. Realizing she still sat there staring at him, she quickly stood and shook his hand.

Her palm tingled where it met his. She looked at him and her smile became a full-fledged grin.

"Thank you. I promise that you won't be dissatisfied."

He stared at her for a few seconds, not loosening his grip.

"I'm sure I won't," he said before releasing her hand and sitting back down, to turn to his computer. "Speak to Marie on your way out. She'll see about getting you access to the necessary files and meeting the rest of the team."

"Of course. No problem." She bent to pick up her bag. When she glanced back up, he was already busy back at work, looking through his email client and responding to messages.

I guess I've been dismissed. She turned to leave.

"Ms. James..."

"Yes?" she replied, stopping in her tracks

and turning back to face him.

"I want a full analysis, scope of work, and project timeline in my hands by the end of the week."

"Not a problem," she said with a smirk as she turned and continued out of his office.

CHAPTER | THREE

Eight weeks later, Veronica was back in Rossi's waiting room swinging her crossed leg impatiently. He was late. Again. Sadly, after working with him for the past two months, Veronica had grown used to his tardiness.

In all honesty, she couldn't really fault him. The man ran a multimillion-dollar company and held meetings at all hours of the day and night. She understood that her concerns and emergencies were just part of a much longer running list that he dealt with on a daily basis. However, glancing down at her cell phone to check the time, she struggled not to let her impatience get the better of her.

She was keen to meet with Rossi and discuss her progress on the project. Tucking a stray curl behind her ear, she tried to ignore the fluttering of her stomach, telling herself she was just eager to go over the progress of the project.

But the fluttering had nothing to do with the meeting, but with Rossi himself. She paused her swinging leg and shook her head.

"Be honest." She tsked softly.

It was more than impatience—she was excited to see Rossi again period.

Veronica was honest enough with herself to admit she found the bossy CEO sexy. She would have to be deaf, blind, and the most hardcore lesbian on earth not to find him attractive. The man just plain oozed sensuality.

Working in a predominantly male-dominated field, she had always made sure to never mix business with pleasure. There had been enough difficulty proving her expertise without people insinuating any strides she made were due to her skills in bed.

Before working with Rossi, she'd never been tempted to re-evaluate her personal rules, and unfortunately, this project was too important for her to let a little attraction stand in her way. Not to mention the enormous task she faced in completing within the projected period.

She sighed and resumed swinging her leg as she thought of all the time she had already spent on the project and the work she knew was still left to be done.

After countless hours staring at and rewriting bad programming code, Veronica was convinced the previous lead programmer for the Niles Enterprises project was a con artist and a hack.

She'd spent the first few days deciphering the tangled web of shitty code and reports the man had left behind. As best as she could tell, he'd produced a labyrinth of smoke and mirrors meant to convince Rossi the project was progressing.

She'd already spent several hours interviewing the remaining team of programmers trying to discern how deep the deception ran.

It was obvious that the previous lead had hired a team of entry level and junior programmers that were either too novice to catch the deception, or too naive to not question obvious bad coding choices. However, after speaking with the team and working with them for several weeks, she was confident they were capable of moving forward and completing the project. They just needed guidance and organization, and, despite all of the problems she found with the project, Veronica was still confident she could deliver on her promise to Rossi.

During their first meeting together after she was hired onto the project, she had promised Rossi a twelve week time-line for completion, and she was well on her way to getting there. She had already spent countless sleepless nights ensuring that the final product would not only meet Rossi's expectations, but exceed them as well.

She had a lot riding on this deal and couldn't afford to fail. She also admitted to herself that some part of her wanted to impress her boss on a personal level. For her, delivering an amazing product was the closest she'd ever come to a flirty smile and flash of leg.

Even to her subconscious mind, that sounded pathetic.

Glancing around the empty waiting room, she was tempted to leave and just send Rossi an email detailing her current progress. Despite her excitement to show him the latest improvements, this would save her from one more uncomfortable session in his office where she tried to concentrate on business and not think about her attraction for him.

When she'd first started on the project, she'd been surprised he insisted on so many face-to-face meetings.

Truthfully, at the beginning, the in-person appointments were incredibly helpful. Aside from being able to really work through his expectations for CLEO, they gave her the chance to get a peek at how the enigmatic CEO's mind worked.

Unfortunately, after the first few times, the meetings became more like lessons in torture. She found herself constantly repeating to herself mentally that it would be highly unprofessional to straddle her client and put to rest her theories of how good his mouth might feel against hers.

It had become somewhat embarrassing to her highly focused mind to be constantly distracted by definitively naughty thoughts whenever she was in the same room with the man. It had gotten to the point where she began solving calculus problems in her head whenever she found herself veering off to the realm of *no way, no how.*

Being forced to wait indefinitely each time before each meeting didn't help her jittery nerves, or more embarrassingly, her damp panties.

She was at the point where she was seriously considering investing in an actual Calculus text book, or perhaps, even flashcards.

Checking the time once more, she made the decision to just leave her report on Rossi's desk and send him a follow-up email.

Standing, she glanced quickly down the hall, making sure his assistant was still nowhere to be seen.

She quickly made her way to Rossi's massive office and placed her report in the center of his desk. She was about to leave when she decided to double check that the correct screen shot photos were included on one of the report pages.

Despite the fact that she knew she was being a chicken by not wanting to meet with Rossi in person, she still wanted to make sure he was wowed by her progress. She had just placed the report back on the desk when she heard voices coming from the waiting area, Rossi's deep baritone unmistakable.

Veronica could only assume that after weeks of lust-induced stress, her brain had a temporary malfunction, because instead of taking a seat and calmly waiting for him to enter the office, she quickly sprinted to the sofa across room and kneeled behind it.

As soon as she felt her knee hit the floor, she was shaking her head at the stupidity of her action.

Just because she was avoiding the man didn't mean she had to hide behind actual furniture when he was around. She was about to rise when he entered the room, speaking to his assistant across his shoulder.

"I'm sorry, sir. Ms. James was here just a few minutes ago," Marie stated.

"Don't worry about it. It looks like she left her report here for me. I wasn't expecting to be over an hour late. Even I don't expect people to wait for me this long," he replied.

She held her breath and took a peek around the edge of the couch. She saw him standing behind his desk, yanking off his tie and suit jacket while Marie stood at the doorway.

"Go ahead and call it a night. I'm going to give this report a quick once over and head home myself."

"Alright, I'll see you in the morning. Goodnight." Marie turned to leave.

Veronica watched Marie close the door in growing horror. She could hear the woman packing up her desk and leaving the outer office, and with it, any chance of her crawling out of the room undetected.

There was no way for her to make a graceful appearance. What could she say?

"Oh. Hi there! I was just checking for spider webs and dust bunnies?"

She inwardly groaned as she ducked her head back behind the couch and hoped that Rossi would read through her report quickly and leave. She could escape once he left, she told herself desperately. Staying crouched behind the couch, she prayed he was as tired as he'd sounded when he'd walked in and would leave quickly.

CHAPTER | FOUR

Victor leaned back in his chair, closed his eyes, and exhaled deeply. It had been one hellishly long day.

He'd stayed up later than he wanted the night before to conduct a teleconference with some potential Russian investors, and came in early that morning to deal with a construction crisis involving a new South Beach development that was already behind schedule.

He was exhausted and glad the day was finally over, but glancing down at the file on his desk, he couldn't help but feel disappointed that he hadn't been able to meet with Veronica that afternoon.

Sniffing, he could still smell her scent in the room. Whenever she was around, there hung a faint hint of coconut, honey, and just plain Veronica in the air. A heady combination that always had him thinking of wet pussy and sweaty sex.

He didn't know why he kept torturing himself with their weekly meetings. He was semi-hard every time she entered his office and rock hard by the time she left.

If it weren't for the importance of the application she was working on and the flashing, hands-off signals she seemed to always display, he would have made a play for her weeks ago. Unfortunately, he did not tread where he wasn't wanted.

"What a shame," he mumbled to himself as he loosened the top few buttons of his shirt.

Veronica was smart, snarky, funny, and sexy as hell. The type of woman he usually avoided like the plague—the kind he couldn't be casual with. She was smart enough to capture his attention and comfortable enough with herself and in her skills to speak her mind and not pull any punches. She wouldn't be demanding of his time, but she would know if he no longer wanted to give it.

Veronica was the type of woman any man would want to keep happy, but he usually wasn't the type to be held down. Yet, she tempted him enough to want to give an actual *real* relationship a try. Suddenly, having someone to wake up to and be demanding of his time didn't sound like such a death sentence.

He relaxed further into his chair, remembering their last meeting.

She'd worn her customary boxy slacks and a loose shirt, and as usual, Victor had tortured himself trying to imagine what kind of curves her clothing hid from him. That had become one of his favorite games while he listened to her husky voice talk about code compilation and server space.

He was at the point where he was theorizing about the size of her nipples when she excitedly jumped up from her chair and walked over to the large screen television he used as a monitor on the opposite end of the room.

"The new dashboard is finally up and running," she said excitedly as she leaned forward and stuck a small flash drive into the side port of the screen. "I wanted you to see what it would look like live and on screen and not just some print out on paper."

In truth, he couldn't really remember what images flashed across the large screen. All he could remember was the flash of lace-covered breast he'd glimpsed when she'd leaned over to insert the flash drive. All he could see at that moment as Veronica continued on about the usefulness of the new feature were her large, caramel, smooth breasts tipped with perfect, chocolate-colored nipples.

Thinking back now, he wasn't quite sure how he had gotten through that last meeting without grabbing her and nuzzling his head between her perfect tits.

Groaning out loud, he reached down and rubbed his cock through his pants. He was a breast man through and through, and the glimpse he'd received that day had been haunting his fantasies ever since.

He had gotten to the point of where he was constantly imagining Veronica walking into his office wearing a pair of her sex-personified heels and stripping for him. Slowly revealing all of the luscious skin she kept so well hidden.

He fantasized about her leaning over him and feeding him her breasts as she straddled him on his chair and rode his cock until he exploded.

Groaning again, Victor glanced at the closed door and began unbuckling his pants. Taking his straining cock into his hands, he sighed as he stroked himself, thinking of all the things he wanted to do to a naked and willing Veronica James.

Veronica huddled behind the couch, worrying over Rossi's response to her latest report. She heard him groan several times and grew worried he may not like some of the upgrades she made to the application. They were ambitious changes, but also completely necessary for the application to be as robust and flexible as the boss requested.

She was nibbling on her lower lip, debating on whether she should take another quick peek around the couch to gauge his expression while he was reading her report, when she heard the distinct sound of a zipper being lowered and a relieved sigh drifting through the air.

Her breath caught at the implications of the sound.

Is he getting undressed, she asked herself as her heart rate began to gallop in earnest. She smothered a soft moan as the thought of an undressed Rossi so close to her settled in her mind. *Of course he's not,* she lectured to herself and shook her head to shake out of her lust-induced haze.

Still, she couldn't resist taking a peek.

Taking a quick breath, she leaned forward and looked over the corner of the couch. Her

Laurel Cremant

breath froze in her chest and her eyes widened as she took in the sight before her.

Rossi sat leaning back in his big executive chair, his head thrown back, eyes closed, and with his hand caressing the most magnificent cock she'd ever seen.

Veronica couldn't look away. Her gaze was completely riveted to the sight of him, slowly touching himself up and down. His penis was long and thick with arousal.

His movements held her in rapt attention, as his fist tightened around his shaft with each upward stroke. When he rubbed his thumb across the tip and slicked pearly beads of pre-cum around the bulbous head, she struggled to hold back a whimper.

She wanted to crawl across the room and help him smooth the droplets with her tongue and suck him whole. She watched as he increased the tempo of his pumping fist and she struggled to breathe. She'd never considered herself a voyeur, but watching Rossi get himself off was the most erotic thing she'd ever seen.

Her mouth had gone dry and she quickly ran her tongue along her lips, wishing they were on him, wrapped around his pulsing dick.

She had a fleeting thought that her attraction to Rossi had finally pushed her over to the deep end, from lustful thoughts to downright dirty and raunchy need. Her breath was coming out in pants and her panties had surpassed *damp* the moment she first looked and saw him stroking himself.

She couldn't make herself turn away. She was entranced, wanting, and needing to see him reach his release. His tempo slowed a bit, as if he was trying to prolong the moment, trying to torture her with the view of his dick pulsing for release. He rubbed his thumb across the engorged tip again and began pumping his fist in earnest.

Veronica's ears began to ring as she waited in anticipation. She stuck her tongue out again to moisten her lips as she saw his hand tighten and his dick flush a deep purple as he came, the pearly ropes of cum drizzling over his hand and down to his ball sack.

Her throat constricted as she imagined those milky drops sliding down her throat.

It took a moment for her to realize her ears were still ringing.

It took her another moment to realize the ringing wasn't in her ears, but the melodic tingling of a cell phone.

It took an even longer moment for her to realize the sound came from her own cell phone that rang loudly into the air.

In a flash, she looked up, dragging her gaze from Rossi's convulsing cock to see his eyes locked on her from across the room as the phone let loose its final tone.

CHAPTER | FIVE

hen Victor first heard the ringing of a phone, he thought it was his own, too caught up in his pleasure to realize that the sound came from across the room. When the discrepancy finally registered, he snapped his eyes open, briefly pausing his pumping fist, searching out for the sound, only to see Veronica staring intently at his dick.

He couldn't take his eyes away from her.

She was crouched across the room, her body mostly hidden behind his couch, but he could see her face clearly.

And what he saw was lust clearly stamped across her beautiful features.

Her light-brown cheeks were flushed, her lips wet and pouty, and her eyes had a slumberous quality to them that threw him over the edge.

She was so focused on his dick she didn't seem to notice him staring right at her. He couldn't stop his hand from renewing the firm pumping on his shaft. He felt his balls draw up and his seed roll up his dick as her perfect pink tongue peeked out of her mouth and slicked across her pouty lips.

He came in his hand watching her lick her lips and pant across the room. He came wishing she was kneeling between his legs sucking him dry.

In the moments following his release, he waited to feel some sort of embarrassment or shame about being caught masturbating in his own office, but as he stared across the room at the look of lust on her face, he felt his dick twitch in his hand, ready for another round. *No*, he thought to himself, *this is a definite game changer*. Calm and cool Veronica James was just as attracted to him as he was to her.

He watched as awareness of his stare slowly dawned on her face. When she snapped her eyes to his, he felt his dick harden further.

"Fuck," she whispered softly into the now silent room.

Expecting to see him flinch away in

anger, Veronica was surprised when Rossi calmly reached across his desk for some tissues and slowly began to clean himself.

"I believe I just did that," he said, quirking an eyebrow at her. "The question is, why did I have an audience?"

It wasn't until he began to tuck his member away and zip up his pants that her muscles finally relinquished control back to her brain.

She scrambled up to her feet as Rossi stood from his chair and began to walk over to her.

"This isn't what it looks like," she said, her voice coming out in an embarrassing squeak as she scrambled back towards the door and away from his stalking gait. "I... I was just going to drop my report and was about to leave when..."

Her voice trailed off as she struggled to come up with a plausible excuse for her presence in his office.

"When you had an urge to hide behind my couch?" Rossi asked in a dry tone as he leaned forward to place his hand against the door and effectively trapped her against it.

"Yes! I mean, no. That's not what happened," she stammered as she pressed her back against the panel and fumbled for the knob. "I was going to leave, I swear. I didn't intend..."

"To take in a show, instead." He chuckled

softly.

"Uh no, but I didn't see anything," she said.

"Really," she stated at his raised brow.

"You understand how this situation changes this relationship, don't you?" he asked, pulling back from her and placing his hands in his pocket.

He rocked back on his heels and studied her. She hoped he couldn't see the rising panic she was feeling reflected on her face.

"No," Veronica exclaimed. She felt her eyes widen to the point that they may pop from their sockets as she ceased her struggle with the door knob. "No," she repeated, shaking her head. "This doesn't change anything."

"I don't see how it doesn't," he replied.

"The application is almost finished," she went on, ignoring his comment. "You can't fire me now. We have a contract."

"You have to agree that the dynamic here has changed." He slowly shook his head at her.

"It doesn't have to," she insisted. "We can just pretend this never happened. It doesn't change anything."

"I don't really see—"

"I'm serious. We can just wipe the slate clean. The first presentation to the VPs is tomorrow, and the application is halfway done."

Victor tuned out the rest of Veronica's rambling and stared into her eyes, seeing the desperation behind her words. She was assuming he wanted to end their professional relationship. But that was far from the truth.

She had saved the company and regardless of the current situation, he was enough of a business man to not let it interfere with completing the project. Too much time and money had been invested, and regardless of his attraction to her, he had every intention of offering her a retainer position with his firm.

She was extremely bright and focused. He would be a fool to not recognize such obvious talent. However, she didn't seem to see that. Thinking he could use this to his advantage, he held up a hand to silence her, and chose his words carefully.

"Tomorrow's meeting is cancelled," he said sternly.

"But—" Veronica rushed to interrupt.

"I won't end your contract just yet," he continued as if she hadn't spoken. "The company has waited this long for the application; we can wait an additional week. I need some time to decide whether I still want to move forward with having you lead the team."

He turned to walk back to his desk. As he sat down, he stared at her from across the room. She seemed rooted to the floor, with a look of pure panic on her face.

"I don't appreciate being spied on, Ms. James," he said when it looked like she would speak again.

He watched as she firmed her lips into a tight line. He could see a spark of anger flare in her eyes as she clenched her fists at her side. *Fuck, but she is hot when she's angry*, he thought, resisting the urge to stroke himself through his pants.

"I need to decide if this working relationship can be salvaged," he added, gathering his papers and leaning down to grab his briefcase. "Until then, I suggest you make yourself scarce and try to curb your voyeur tendencies."

As he strode towards the door, he paused in front of her and slowly ran his free hand up her arm, before he gently moved her to the side.

46

"I'll be in touch regarding the status of your contract," he said as he opened the door and strode out of the office.

CHAPTER | SIX

Veronica Awoke the next morning groggy, disoriented, and horny as hell. She struggled to hold onto a dream that featured Victor Rossi and a bowl of ice cream.

She snuggled a pillow to her stomach, hoping to return to the fantasy, when the events of the prior night crashed through her psyche.

"Shit," she yelped out as she shot up to a sitting position.

She whimpered as the room began to swim around her and the contents of her stomach began to roll around in earnest. Clutching her aching head, she glanced around the room and saw an empty bottle of rum sitting on her nightstand alongside several empty beer bottles and empty chocolate bar wrappers.

Looking down, she saw she was still dressed in her clothes from the previous day. They were rumpled and stained with what looked like streaks of chocolate. Well, she hoped they were chocolate. She wiggled her toes and felt a lone shoe dangle from her right foot.

"Shit," she repeated as she lay her head back down gingerly on her pillow. She wanted to pull her covers over her head as the events of the previous night played through her head over and over again.

She barely recalled collecting her things and making her way home, but she vividly remembered Rossi pleasuring himself, and the disastrous end to her presence in his office.

She couldn't believe she had let her stupid attraction to him jeopardize the project. Even now, knowing it would take her months to recover financially from the loss of his account, she remained aroused by what she had seen.

"You're pathetic," she mumbled into the empty room. She slowly sat back up and swung her legs over the side of her queen-sized bed.

She toed off her remaining shoe and stood carefully. Bracing herself mentally, she made her way to the bathroom, removing her clothes along the way. She wobbled into the shower stall and turned the cold water on blast.

She stood shivering under the stinging spray of water, waiting for her head to stop spinning and her jumbled thoughts to settle. *I need a game plan*, she thought as her brain eventually stopped its chaotic panic.

She reached to turn on the hot water and let the growing steam in the shower relax her tense muscles.

She'd dealt with bad situations before when she was in New York. Admittedly, none of them had involved her watching a colleague or superior in a compromising position, but she had survived. In the end, her work had always spoken for itself. She just needed to convince Rossi that, regardless of the situation, she was the best person to complete the project.

She shook her head and admitted to herself that the chances of the boss choosing to keep her contract were slim to none. Best case scenario was that even if she couldn't count on him as a reference in the future, she could still use her work with him in her portfolio. She groaned softly into the steamed enclosure.

She needed to concentrate on being solvent, which meant nixing her plans to hire a junior developer. She would have to put her ear to the ground and pick up several smaller accounts to just even things out from the loss of Rossi's business. There was no telling when she'd be able to land another account as large as his.

Firming her lips in determination, she reached out and turned off the water. Veronica reached for a towel and began to briskly rub herself down.

"It's not the end of the world," she said bravely as she stepped out of the shower.

She walked back into her bedroom feeling a little more human and a little more prepared to deal with the situation. Within minutes, she was dressed and sitting at her computer, updating her portfolio, when she heard the light chime notifying her that an email just hit her inbox. She glanced at the edge of her monitor and her breath caught when she saw Rossi's name in the message box.

She hesitated before clicking on the blinking icon. The effects of the pep talk she gave herself earlier quickly disappeared.

It was one thing to plan for the worse, and another to actually have to live through it. Taking a deep breath, she clicked on the message. It consisted of only two sentences.

The presentation is back on for today. Meet

me briefly at 3:30 prior to the presentation to discuss the new terms of your contract.
~Victor

Veronica released a huge sigh of relief. It looked like she wasn't going to lose the account, after all. She crinkled her brow briefly as she read the message again.

"New terms," she mumbled out loud. "What the hell does that mean?" she said into the empty room.

CHAPTER | SEVEN

Victor sat in his chair, waiting for
Veronica to arrive. He'd spent most of
the night devising the perfect plan.

He'd thought of just asking her out,
which was the sane and rational thing to do, he
admitted. However, whenever he thought of the
look of lust on her face and the weeks of the
hands-off signals she had thrown his way, he
decided a few more drastic measures were
called for.

After weeks of fantasizing about her, he
wanted Veronica to admit her attraction to him.
And if he got to live out a few of his own
fantasies along the way, so be it, he thought
smugly. He felt himself get hard at the
possibilities.

"Down, boy," he muttered to his crotch.

He needed this meeting with her to go
smoothly. He couldn't reveal any hint of
attraction, especially considering the "new

terms" he planned on negotiating.

The soft beep of his intercom interrupted his thoughts, and his assistant's smooth voice filled the air.

"Ms. James is here to see you."

He took a quick breath and reached for his intercom.

"Send her in," he said. *Time to play,* he thought as he schooled his features into a blank mask.

He leaned back in his chair with his hands steepled and waited as Marie ushered Veronica into the room and closed the door.

When he got his first glimpse of her, he struggled not to let his surprise or lust show on his face. During the weeks they'd worked together, he had never seen her in anything remotely considered figure-hugging, let alone in any colors other than black, gray, and white.

But today was a different story.

She strode into his office wearing a long, purple pencil skirt that ended just past her knees, and a white, scoop-necked shirt that molded her breasts and ended just at her hips, with a slim purple belt cinched in at her waist. He fought down a groan as his gaze reached her feet.

As usual, her choice of shoes didn't disappoint. They were constructed of a black stiletto heel with a multitude of thin black and purple straps crisscrossing across her feet and ending with a purple bow at her ankle.

He could come just watching her walk around in those shoes. The woman was turning him into a freak and he loved every minute of it.

"Have a seat," he said briskly leaning forward. "We have a lot to cover."

Veronica struggled not to appear nervous. She'd taken a lot of care that morning dressing for this meeting, deciding to wear what she deemed her "power suit." She usually preferred her more comfortable pant suits, but she kept this particular outfit for the times she needed to feel an extra boost of confidence. If ever there was a day that she needed that confidence, it was today.

She walked briskly to Rossi's desk and sat down. She tried to gauge his mood, but his features were a blank mask. *Crap*, she thought, cringing inwardly. Over the last few weeks, she had gotten used to him looking at her with a friendly smile or quirky grin. The blank look he was giving her now was disconcerting. She knew it was to be expected considering the situation, but a part of her couldn't help but feel hurt by his expression.

"I'm glad to hear you re-thought the decision to cancel the meeting today. I promise, you won't be disappointed," she began briskly.

"Oh, I know I won't be," Rossi replied as he pushed a stack of paper towards her. "This is a contract for permanent retainer services with Niles Enterprises. You will be free to take on as many side accounts as you'd like, but when dealing with our projects, there will be complete exclusivity."

Veronica was speechless. She sat silent for a moment, letting his words sink in as she stared down at the dollar amount on the contract. Enough for her to stay in the black for the rest of the year and hire *two* junior developers, not just one.

"Mr. Rossi, I—" she finally managed to sputter out.

"Please, call me Victor," he interrupted. "I think after last night we can at least be on a first name basis."

"Umm, okay... Victor," she said, trying hard to contain her blush at the mention of the previous night. "Last night is already forgotten. I can't wait to move forward on this project with you." She aimed a bright smile at him.

"I'm afraid you're mistaken," Rossi said. "The events from last night are far from forgotten, and I seriously doubt they ever will be."

He stated the words flatly, his mouth thinning into a grim line.

Her smile dimmed. She looked down at the retainer contract he placed in front of her.

"I don't understand," she said. "If you're not willing to forget, then why offer me a retainer contract?"

Her confusion sounded obvious in her voice.

"I consider myself a damn good business man," he responded. "I learned a long time ago to not overlook talent, and you're a very talented woman, Veronica. I would be fool to let you go when your skill is an obvious asset to me and my company."

She released a silent breath as relief slowly worked its way through her system.

"Thank you. I'll take this home with me and look it over. From what you've said, it sounds more than fair," she said, tapping the contract in front of her while trying to look cool.

"I think you may want to hear the rest of my

terms before taking that home," he continued.

"I'm sure that whatever they are, we can negotiate something amicable for both of us," she replied, smiling again and feeling much more confident.

This meeting was turning out much better than she ever could have expected.

For the amount of money Ros— Victor was willing to pay her for a retainer, she was sure she could work with any additional terms he wanted to set. It was just so hard to read him. His expression was still closed off, despite his praise of her talent.

"One of the first lessons I learned in business is that, when I walk into any meeting or any type of negotiation, I need to have the upper hand before even stepping into the room. Without that upper hand, I would always be forced to settle for a compromise beyond my comfort zone," he said before pausing to stare at her expectantly.

"I could see how that would be important," she said quickly to fill the silence.

"Good." He cracked the barest of smiles at her. "So you can understand how what

60

happened last night would distress me on more than one level."

"I don't see—"

"You saw me in a vulnerable position," he said, cutting into her response. "At this moment, just knowing that gives you the upper hand, and the only way I plan on continuing our relationship is to take it back."

Veronica chose her words carefully. There was a gleam that shone through his eyes when he spoke now that was beginning to make her uneasy.

It was obvious there was nothing she could say to convince him that what happened last night could be forgotten. She even agreed with him, but she couldn't tell him that. With a retainer contract on the line, she had too much to lose. She took a calm breath, licked her dry lips, and cleared her throat before speaking.

"How, exactly, do you plan on doing that?" she asked.

"By tilting the odds back in my favor," he said, leaning back in his chair and giving her his first genuine smile since she walked into the room. "To be perfectly blunt, Veronica, last night you saw mine, now it's time for you to show me yours."

She was pretty sure she was doing a damn

good impersonation of a gold fish at that moment. There was no way she could have heard him right. Victor Rossi did not just ask her to *show him hers*. *No way, no how*.

"Excuse me?" she asked. The question sounded lame even to her ears. She cleared her throat and tried again. "You can't be serious."

"Oh, I'm definitely serious."

"This isn't grade school. You can't just ask me to drop my pants just because I got a look at you in a compromising position," she exclaimed.

"Oh, I'm not asking you to drop your pants."

"You're not?"

She had another moment of relief before he leaned forward and spoke again.

"I want you to pull up your skirt, take off your panties, and hand them over to me," he said, holding her shocked gaze. "And I want you to do that every time you meet with me. I want the knowledge that you're laid as bare as I was last night."

"You're crazy," she exclaimed. She didn't bother trying to hide her anger. What type of person went around demanding panties as retribution? "I'm not going to hand anything over to you except my foot up your—"

"Think really hard before you refuse this contract. You saw me in more than just a compromising position last night, Veronica. Just be glad that I'm not asking you to put on a reciprocal show," he interrupted harshly.

"This is blackmail," she spat out.

"Semantics," he responded coolly.

She sat in angry silence for several minutes just staring at him. The man was completely insane. She dropped her gaze to the retainer contract.

She wanted badly to just get up and walk away, but he was right. The money from the contract was hard to ignore. The retainer alone was a big boon, but to have a company as large as Niles Enterprises in her portfolio was a huge deal. It gave her business a level of legitimacy that would otherwise have taken her several years to obtain.

She stared down at the contract a few minutes more before she made her final decision. In the end, it all came down to how badly she wanted her business to succeed. She would agree to Victor's insane demand, but not without stating some ground rules of her own.

With her decision made, she straightened her back and locked her gaze firmly onto his cold green eyes.

"I won't sleep with you," she said calmly.

"I don't believe I asked for that pleasure," he replied, quirking his eyebrow in a way that she was finding increasingly annoying.

She pressed her lips together firmly. He was behaving like a jackass. She couldn't believe she had spent all that time fantasizing about such a ruthless jerk.

"And no one else will be aware of this... arrangement except the two of us," she continued.

"I've never been one to discuss private business matters with outside parties," he said with a slight smile playing across his lips.

"Fine," she said as she dropped her gaze from his and reached into her purse to pull out a pen. She pulled the contract forward and signed the bottom page with hands she fought to keep steady from shaking. After she placed the pen down, she couldn't prevent her hands from clutching tightly onto the cool glass top of Victor's desk.

She pulled in a shaky breath and raised her gaze back to his, her eyes steady on him as she pushed back her chair and began to raise her skirt.

"Not so fast," he said harshly, his words halting her movement.

She let her skirt fall back down to her knees. For a split second, she again thought that he had changed his mind. But his eyes remained cold and she knew that wasn't the case.

"The deal is that you would show me yours, so come here," he said, gesturing to his side of the desk.

If it weren't for his cold regard, Veronica almost believed his voice had grown huskier. She locked her knees to keep them from trembling as she made her way around his desk.

"Continue," he said when she reached his chair.

She watched and struggled hard not to reach out and slap his smirking face as he leaned back in his chair and rested his folded hands across his flat stomach.

Veronica felt her knees tremble and her stomach quaver at his focused stare and tried not to let her surprise at her body's reaction show.

As pissed off as she was at his demands, it seemed as if her body had yet to receive the message that the recent object of her obsession had turned from a sexy crush to an arrogant ass. Even now, standing in front of him about to submit to his ludicrous demand, she couldn't keep a warm flush from spreading throughout her body, and a lick of desire settle in her stomach.

She didn't know who she was angrier with at this point—herself for being so aroused, or Victor for putting her in such a demeaning position.

"Sometime this century, please," he said arrogantly. He no longer looked in her eyes. Instead, he kept his eyes fixed squarely below her waist.

Steeling herself against the need to physically hurt him, she kept her gaze trained on him as she clasped her skirt in her fists and pulled it up to her waist. She saw him stiffen and hoped he was just as uncomfortable as she was.

She held her skirt up with one hand and reached down to hook her fingers into the elastic of her blue lace thong with the other. She paused only briefly before pulling it down over her hips and releasing her fingers to let the patch of lace pool at her feet.

She was about to smooth her skirt back down over her hips when Victor reached forward in a flash and grabbed her hips firmly in his hands.

"I gave you more than just a few seconds worth of a look last night," he said huskily. "I'm pretty sure I'm owed more than just a quick peek now," he added as he moved her over slightly.

The cool glass top of his desk grazed her ass as he shifted her over. Her muscles felt frozen. The moment his hands clasped her hips, she felt such a rush of heat she was afraid to speak. It burned so quickly, she struggled to keep it from fogging up her mind completely.

She stood quietly, locked in a shocked haze of heat, as he leaned her back against his desk. The movement caused her legs to splay open slightly, just enough to give him a full view of her pussy.

He stroked his thumbs across her hips and down, slowly, to the crease of her inner thighs. He kept his touch light, his fingers never brushing the aching juncture between her legs.

"I wouldn't have figured you for the clean-shaven look," he murmured.

His softly spoken words jolted her out of her frozen state. She stiffened abruptly and straightened away from the desk.

"Fuck you," she said as she shoved his hands away and smoothed her skirt back down to her knees.

She marched back around to the other side of the desk and crossed her arms protectively around her chest.

"The VPs have arrived, sir," Marie's disembodied voice came into the room.

Victor reached across his desk and pressed the intercom button. "Go ahead and show them in," he said smoothly.

Veronica watched as he swiveled his chair to the side and leaned forward to grasp something from the floor. She bit back an outraged shriek when he straightened up and she saw he held her blue thong in his hand. He rolled it up quickly and stuffed it into the inside pocket of his suit jacket. He chuckled huskily at her outraged look.

"It's show time," he said softly enough for her only her ears as Marie ushered in the executives for the demo presentation.

CHAPTER | EIGHT

S everal hours later, Veronica was trying hard to pull herself out of the rabbit hole that had become her life. She sat at a private table nursing an amaretto sour in one of downtown Miami's most posh restaurants.

Normally, she would be happy to be sipping a drink after a long and stressful day. Unfortunately, she wasn't by herself or surrounded by friends. Instead, she sat panty-less surrounded by Victor Rossi and the VPs of Niles Enterprises.

No amount of alcohol in the world could make the situation less uncomfortable. She knew because, since they arrived at the restaurant after her presentation, she'd begun trying to drown out her frustration with liquor.

At times like these, she cursed her Haitian ancestry. She often joked with her friends that rum was such a staple in her country's diet that it would take more than a gallon of alcohol to get her good and drunk. And that wasn't really far from the truth.

She was on her tenth drink and only had the slightest of buzzes. With a frown at her current glass, she figured she would have to stop soon before she got liver poisoning. She shifted in her seat to uncross and re-cross her legs while trying hard not to blush when the motion reminded her of her *in flagrante* state.

Unfortunately, when she shifted, her thighs lightly brushed against Rossi, who'd somehow managed to seat himself next to her when they first arrived at the restaurant.

She gritted her teeth and resisted the urge to turn and scowl at him.

He was completely to blame for her miserable mood. In the course of one afternoon, he had managed to save her business and ruin her mental health, all with one request.

Now it's time for you to show me yours.

She gave a mental snort.

Ignoring her earlier decision to stop drinking, she raised her glass to her lips and downed the rest of the clear, burning liquid.

"If this project continues to stay within the timelines, we should have no problem pushing this out to all of our properties by the end of the year."

Veronica swiveled her head to look at Adrian Garcia, Ross's VP of Finance. The man had been in an excited mood ever since they left the office. The others nodded and continued to speak excitedly to each other.

Under normal circumstances, she would be enjoying herself and basking in the praise the VPs heaped on her. After she'd completed her presentation, they'd expressed how pleased they were with her progress. Apparently, the company was poised to take over a large property management firm in Georgia named Continental.

A key factor in the takeover timeline was how quickly Niles Enterprises could integrate Continental's finance and accounting department with their own. The new features she recently added to the application would make that integration virtually seamless.

When someone suggested they go out to celebrate, she'd tried to excuse herself, but Victor had insisted she attend. She'd briefly considered arguing with him, but the excitement of the VPs and the hard look in his eyes had told her to save her energy.

Thankfully, the restaurant was only a short walk from the building that housed Niles Enterprises. The moment they arrived, the group got ushered into a private section of the restaurant with the VIP treatment.

The service they received didn't surprise her. If anything, it served to increase her anger, reminding her that Rossi was a rich man used to people tripping all over themselves to please him.

Thinking it about it now had her clenching her right fist tight and signaling the waiter with the other. The man approached eagerly.

She was about to request another dink when she felt a warm hand land on her thigh; she stiffened. Before she could turn and rip Rossi a new orifice, his warm breath teased her earlobe.

"Don't you think you've had enough to drink?" he whispered softly.

Veronica turned to flash him a sugary-sweet smile.

"No, I haven't," she said calmly, then turned back to the waiter and placed her order. "Barbancourt on the rocks, please, and make it a double," she said to the waiting young man.

The meandering hand squeezed her thigh tightly before his grip loosened. She turned back to face him and leaned in, her gaze glued to his.

"Remove the hand, slick," she whispered, not bothering to hide her annoyance.

Instead of removing the offending hand, he began to move it up and down her thigh in slow, sweeping movements.

"Hmmm," he replied back as he chuckled softly. "I don't feel like it."

She was barely able to hold back an outraged shriek. The man was too arrogant for words. She was about to reply to his taunting comment when the waiter returned with her drink.

To spite him, she lifted the glass to her mouth and finished it in one swallow, her eyes never wavering from his. His lips tightened into a grim line as the rum burned a smooth path down her throat to settle with a warm caress in her stomach.

As the warmth spread through her belly, she finally began to feel the faint, fuzzy glow of tipsiness. She swiveled her head back to the celebratory crowd and smiled warmly at

Adrian.

"I'm glad you're happy with what I've done so far," she said.

Adrian focused back in on her and gave her a wide charming smile. "You have no idea how much work this application will save us."

Adrian was the one tolerable spot in her afternoon. Aside from being friendly and charming, he had heaped praise upon her and the work she completed on CLEO. It wasn't hard to muster up a genuine smile and respond.

"Just doing my job," she replied.

"Well, that's more than the last guy did," Adrian said derisively as he waggled his eyebrows at her, "I'm pretty sure he just sat around watching *Family Guy* episodes all day."

She couldn't help but laugh at his insight. She had thought the same thing on more than one occasion while trying to decipher the thousands of lines of bad programming code. She felt Rossi shift next to her and turned to see him frown over at Adrian.

"Well, there's still a lot of work to do," he said sternly.

Adrian's smile dimmed only slightly at Rossi's comment. *What a buzz kill.*

"Yes, well, the work will definitely be a lot less frustrating now," Adrian said, regaining his humor. He reached across the table, grabbed Veronica's hand, and stared earnestly into her eyes.

"Marry me, Veronica. I promise to shower you in nothing but the latest technology and trips to Silicon Valley at least once a year," he said jokingly.

She couldn't hold back her snort of laughter. "Sorry, Casanova, but I don't think you can afford the unlimited *Newegg* account I can't live without," she said chuckling, before she withdrew her hand from his.

"Ouch! That hurts," he exclaimed, placing a hand over his heart to feign a heart break.

"Don't you have a meeting with the Continental finance group tomorrow?" Rossi asked in a flat tone.

Surprised, she turned to look at him. For a few moments, she'd almost forgotten he was there. As if reading her thoughts, he ran his hand down her thigh and squeezed her knee hard, causing her to stifle a yelp.

Adrian cleared his throat and she could tell that he was surprised by Rossi's tone as well.

"Yes, we're meeting with their head of finance and lead accountant in the morning."

She barely heard Adrian's response. She was too distracted by Rossi's roaming hand. It moved from her knee and was slowly making its way up her skirt. She tightened her crossed legs, trying to prevent his movements.

She couldn't believe what he was doing and, even worse, she couldn't seem to control her body's response to it, either. The moment she had felt his hand creeping up her leg, her nipples had tightened and she felt desire pool to her center.

He stopped his hand at the top of her inner thigh and began to trace small circles on her flesh, and she fought hard to hold back a moan. Maybe having that last drink wasn't such a good idea, because, as she sat waiting for his hand to move only a few inches higher, she was finding it hard to recall all the reasons why she should hate Victor Rossi.

"Hmmm," he said, his eyes trained on Adrian. "Then you should probably call it an early night. I'll settle the tab and wait until our star programmer here sobers up a bit," he added, smiling slightly to the group.

Recognizing that they had just been dismissed, the VPs made a hasty retreat.

His comment about her needing to sober up was enough to snap her out of her haze. She took deep breaths while she waited for the rest of the group to hurry out of the restaurant.

When they were all gone, she counted to ten, glanced at Rossi's smirking face, and counted to ten one more time before dropping her hand to her lap and grasping his meandering fingers in a tight grip.

"I'm not drunk," she said, wincing only slightly when she heard the slight slurring of her words.

Victor raised a dark eyebrow at her slurred declaration and made no move towards removing his hand from beneath her skirt.

"In the past few hours, I've seen you put enough liquor away to put any frat boy to shame. Whether you believe it or not, you're drunk," he continued, not bothering to hide his smirk.

"Well, if that's the case, wouldn't you consider this taking advantage of me?" She glared at him and then glanced pointedly down at her lap.

"Hmm, you have a point there." He leaned

forward and placed a finger from his free hand beneath her chin, drawing her head up to meet his gaze. "Tell you what – I'll trade you for it."

"Trade me? There's no trade or negotiation here." She glared at him again.

"Come on, Veronica. Where's the fun in that?" He chuckled softly. "How about a friendly drinking game at the very least, or a game of Truth or Dare, instead?"

"Are you on drugs?" she asked scathingly. "What part of your tiny little brain thinks I want to be here right now?"

"Okay, Truth or Dare it is. I'll go first. I choose dare," he said, ignoring her cutting remark.

"How about you just move your hand and I decide not rip you a new ass hole?" She seethed.

"Okay," he said, smiling softly at her.

She felt his hand flex underneath her skirt. She released her grip on him to allow his touch to withdraw.

"Dare accepted," he said.

She saw a gleam brighten his eyes, and before she had a chance to voice a protest, she felt his unhindered hand plunge forward. His fingertips paused for a moment

78

to stroke her smooth nether lips, and she couldn't hold back the aroused whimper that escaped her mouth. She barely held back a moan when he slid a finger into her damp folds and began to slowly brush her clit with light, teasing strokes.

"What are you doing?" she managed to ask in a low, croaking voice.

"Just playing the game."

His gaze flickered across her face, and she felt his hands adjust once more. He replaced his stroking finger with his thumb, and with a slight turn of his wrist, his forefinger slid down her slit to rub just above the rim of her pussy.

"You dared me to move my hand and I did. Now, it's your turn. Truth or dare?" he asked.

Veronica could barely think past the heat blazing through her body. She struggled to take smooth, deep breaths, despite her racing pulse.

"I don't like games," she finally managed to get out in a relatively level voice.

Amusement twitched Rossi's lips upward, and she felt his finger slip past her rim and plunge into her core.

"Truth it is, then," he said while his finger plunged slowly in and out of her. "Why did you stay last night?"

She stared at him with what she was sure

must be a blank look of incomprehension. It was so hard to think past the feel of his fingers in her. She couldn't keep from clenching around his penetration, or her hips from rolling to meet his digits.

Her core begged more of him. She couldn't even muster up her earlier anger. All she could focus on was the pleasure his probing touch gave her.

"Why did you stay?" he repeated, stopping the movement of his thumb and fingers.

"I wanted to leave you the report," she said huskily, desperate for him to resume his ministrations.

He began to rub her clitoris again with his thumb in partial reward to her response. Her breath began to hitch; she was so close to the edge.

Weeks of sexual frustration had left her body hyper-aware. Heat began to prickle at her neck and sliver up and down her back. As much as she wanted the release of orgasm, she fought to hold on to some form of control.

"No, that's why you were there. Why did you *stay*?" he asked again.

Veronica shook her head and pressed her

lips firmly together.

Despite the obvious evidence pooling between her thighs, she refused to voice her attraction for him. She didn't want to admit that the situation wasn't what kept her from leaving; it's what made her stay. The opportunity to see him in such a sexual state had been too tempting to ignore.

She watched him take in the line of her firmed lips and she let out a moan when he plunged two fingers deep into her.

"No truth, then," he said, stroking deep into her with an increased tempo.

He leaned closer over her. His lips were only a breath away from her mouth, and his eyes stared deeply into hers. She licked her lips and braced herself for his reaction to her refusal to respond to his question. She inhaled his scent, a heady mix of earth and spicy vanilla. It engulfed her and she didn't know if she could handle him stopping. Her brain was just too fuzzy with arousal, too consumed with the need to come.

"I guess we're going to have to settle on a dare," he said.

He withdrew his fingers from her core and she let out a small whimper of protest before she felt his forefinger join his thumb to pinch her clitoris.

"Come for me," he demanded before his lips covered hers.

Veronica fisted her hands on his chest and moaned into his mouth as she splintered apart in a wave of pleasure.

CHAPTER | NINE

Victor sat in his car debating how to best deal with a certain Ms. Veronica James. Several weeks had passed since their encounter in the restaurant and he was still struggling to gain some ground with her.

He gripped the steering wheel in frustration as his mind flashed back to that night for what felt like the millionth time. The taste of her mouth as she came apart on his fingers had ingrained itself in his memory. Even now, just the thought of it was enough to make his dick twitch in anticipation. Unfortunately, the moment his lips left hers that night, she'd jumped from her seat and hurried to the rest room.

After several moments of waiting, he'd realized she wasn't going to return to the table. Cursing under his breath, he threw several bills on the table to cover the tab and rushed from the restaurant.

He ran out just in time to see her zip around the corner. He hurried behind her but had enough sense not to approach her. He followed her a few blocks and watched to make sure she got home safely, berating himself the whole way. Not for rushing his seduction, but for being dumb enough to let her leave the table.

Admittedly, he originally planned on taking it slow, teasing her into a confession after a few more panty-less encounters, but he hadn't liked the way Adrian Garcia had flirted with her. Even though he'd only known Veronica a short time, he didn't like the idea of the notorious womanizer getting his hands on her.

When he first stroked her cunt and felt the slippery wetness there, he'd known he wouldn't be able to stop. And after she gushed her release on his fingers, he was sure she was on the verge of confession.

No woman could come apart like that and not admit to the attraction she felt. He let her have her space that night with the intention of resuming full speed at the earliest opportunity, but the sneaky woman had managed to cancel or postpone every meeting he'd scheduled since then.

Victor was getting desperate, and he didn't like the feeling. He'd never really had to work hard to get a woman's attention. He lived in a world where money was just as strong a lure as good looks, and he was blessed with more than his fair share of both. In all honesty, he didn't have to chase Veronica, but something about her drew him.

She had a sharp mind, a quick sense of humor, and never seemed afraid to speak her mind. But it was more than just that. He'd seen her interact with the programming team at Niles. She respected intelligence and always gave the junior staff an opportunity to voice their opinions and suggestions. She was also sexy as hell, and that was driving him crazy.

He found himself imagining what it would be like to come home to her every evening and listen to her quick retorts and snorts of laughter. He imagined sinking his cock into her every night and suckling her breasts every morning, and no matter how many times he imagined it, he never found a variation of the scenes that bored him.

The truth was that he simply wanted her and didn't care why anymore. He wasn't going to let her ignore the possibilities between them, and giving her space no longer worked for him.

Clenching his jaw, he got out of his car and marched into the apartment complex. He was tired of waiting for his woman to come to her senses.

His steps faltered as he replayed the phrase in his head—*his woman*. He liked the sound of that. Whether she liked it or not, Veronica James was going to stop running and be firmly caught by him.

Damn, I feel like shit. Veronica sat in a miserable heap on her couch, surrounded by used tissues and empty bottle boxes of Dayquil. She hated being sick, and this flu had come at the worst possible time.

The completion deadline for CLEO was only a week away, and she still had a few kinks to work out in the code. She'd delegated as much as she could to the programming team at Niles but there was still a lot left for her to do. And as of five minutes ago, she officially had no more energy to spare. Not wanting to fall behind, she had exhausted her supply of Dayquil and continued to work hard into every night instead of resting and giving her body the time it needed to get better.

Unfortunately, her kamikaze work spree

had finally run its course, and she couldn't even spare the energy to crawl to her bed. She used her last store of pitiful strength to close her laptop and return it to her desk before slinking back to her couch, and collapsing onto the deep cushions. Her whole body ached and she couldn't seem to stop shivering. With fondness, her thoughts went to the hot toddies her mom always made when she was sick. She was exhausted, and the thought of the warm elixir was enough to make her tear up and curl up into a ball.

The only good thing about being sick was that it had kept her from thinking about Rossi. Well, most of the time, anyway.

The man, unfortunately, was never too far from her thoughts, and that just pissed her off. She felt heat rush to her face as she remembered the night in the bar and the feel of his fingers stroking inside of her. She couldn't believe she had let him touch her like that. More grating was the fact that she wanted him to do it again.

Her steadfast rule of not mixing business with pleasure was taking a decisive beating. Regardless of her attraction to the arrogant prick, she wouldn't let it go anywhere. Rossi was a typical rich playboy. He had way too much money and way too many women willing to kneel at his feet. Her mind briefly flashed back to the sight of him masturbating in his office, and admittedly, she understood why. The man had a mouthwatering cock.

Shaking her thoughts free of Rossi and his assets, she reminded herself he was most likely just interested in a quick conquest. She had seen men like him work their magic in New York, and she wasn't about to be a player in that game in Miami. *Sleep*, she thought. *I just need a few good hours of sleep and I'll be fine.*

Just as the thought flickered across her mind, she heard a loud knock at her door. Veronica ignored it. She wasn't expecting anyone and no lost delivery man deserved to see her in her state of misery. She couldn't remember when she'd last showered, and her hair had been in the same haphazard pineapple bun on top of her head for days.

The person knocked again and she frowned. Normally, the delivery people for her building didn't bother with more than one attempt. They were usually quick to rap on her door briefly and leave an annoying "*Sorry we missed you*" delivery note stuck to the wood.

"Go away," she managed to croak out.

Her voice was barely louder than a whisper. The person knocked again. Louder this time, and she realized that the sooner she got rid of them, the sooner she could get some much-needed sleep.

Hopefully, the sight of her would be enough to scare them away.

She struggled to swing her legs over to the floor and slowly stood up. The room blurred for a brief second then righted itself, and she made her haltingly to the door. When she finally reached her goal, she paused briefly to lean against it. The short walk had been enough to drain her.

Standing on wobbly legs, she opened the entrance ready to blast whoever stood behind it. Her breath caught in her throat as she stared up into the eyes of Victor Rossi.

"What the hell are *you* doing here?" she demanded, her voice coming out in a scraggy growl.

Victor looked down into Veronica's frowning face and couldn't hold back a smile. Her hair was a disheveled mess with straggled curls sticking out everywhere. She wore a white t-shirt that read "I Heart Dr. Who" and a pair of neon-pink beach shorts. Her face glowed with sweat, and he was pretty sure her nose was running. She looked absolutely adorable.

"I missed you too, sweetie." He grinned at her.

She moved to slam the door in his face, but seemed to stumble when she shifted her weight from the door. He reached out quickly to catch her before she fell.

"Are you okay?" He cradled her against him and felt the heat of her skin sear through his shirt. "Jesus, you're burning up."

He pushed her forward into the apartment and closed the door behind him.

"I'm fine," she mumbled against his chest. "And I'll be even better once you leave, so why don't you just go?" she added weakly.

"That's cute." He scooped her wilting body up into his arms. "Pretending to be all ferocious when you're a limp noodle."

He glanced around the small apartment and began to stride down her single hall searching for her bedroom.

"Put me down," she demanded.

"Give me a second," he said as he headed

to the end of the hall and shoved open the door.

"Have I told you how much I hate you lately?" she groused at him.

"No," he replied as he deposited her gingerly on her bed. "You've been too much of a chicken to speak to me at all, remember?" he teased.

Her mouth fell open in what looked like shock. It was obvious that she hadn't expected him to be so damn blunt. He watched as she clicked her jaw shut and firmed her lips into a mutinous line.

"Hmm, no response to that, huh?" he said.

"Go away." She repeated her earlier request.

"Sorry, that's not going to happen. How long have you been like this?" he asked as he leaned down and felt her forehead.

"I'm fine," she said. "It's just a little cold."

"Veronica, you're burning up. This doesn't feel like just a little cold."

"I don't have a fever," she said. "I'm freezing; ergo, it must be a cold." She looked at him as if he were an idiot.

"I'm sorry to break it to you, but you most definitely have a fever," he said.

"Listen. All I need is a little sleep and I'll be fine. So why don't you just leave so I can get some rest?" she said.

He watched her shiver as she attempted a

wobbly smile. No doubt hoping to cajole him into leaving.

He stared down into her upturned face and just shook his head.

"That was just pathetic. You're going to have to give me more than that pathetic excuse for a smile before you can convince me to leave," he continued as he pushed her back to lie on the bed.

Veronica opened her mouth in an attempt to argue further, he was sure. He held back a smile as her words turned into a shriek of outrage when he began to pull her shirt up her torso.

"What the hell are you doing?" she cried out, her voice coming out in a high-pitched screech. "What are you? Some kind of pervert, getting your rocks off on defenseless miserable women?" she demanded as she struggled against his hands.

Victor resisted the urge to laugh at her accusations. She continued her ranting and he just chose to tune her out.

The truth was that he had no qualms about fucking her in whatever state she was in. He couldn't imagine not wanting to be inside her regardless of her current condition. However, he doubted voicing his opinion would help him at that moment. Instead, he continued to undress her despite her struggles. She was so weak he was able to strip her of her shirt and shorts quickly.

He bit back a groan when he saw that she was wasn't wearing a bra or panties. *Good God, she is fucking beautiful*, he thought as he stared down at her.

His fantasies had not done her body justice. The baggy shirts she favored hid a spectacular pair of breasts. They were big enough to spill out of his large hands and tipped perfectly with dark-purple nipples just made for sucking. Her hips flared out from her waist in rounded invitation and her toned legs led up to the prettiest, most lush pussy he'd ever seen.

His mouth watered as he stared at her cunt until her ranting eventually filtered back into his hearing. She was screeching things about what she planned on doing to his body parts that were enough to dampen his libido. At least long enough to take care of her.

He leaned forward and flipped her limp body over his shoulder and marched into her adjoining bathroom. He leaned her against the bathroom wall and reached into the standing shower and turned on the water.

Veronica continued to blast him with her

caustic tongue until he finally just covered her mouth with his hand and lifted her into the warm shower. She glared at him over his hand.

"Stay here and clean up. The steam should help with the congestion and runny nose. I'll be back in a few minutes. I'm just going to get you something to eat. Then I'm going to help you to bed and you can get some sleep," he said gently.

She stared at him suspiciously for a few moments. He saw the moment she made her decision because her shoulders slumped forward and it looked as if all the fight left her at once. She nodded her head weakly.

Standing in the spray of the shower, she looked like a pathetic drowned rat. A sexy rat, he amended as he flicked his gaze down her wet body. Clearing his throat, he looked up and removed his hand from her mouth.

"I'll be back in a few minutes," he repeated, and left the room.

CHAPTER | TEN

Veronica didn't know what to think of Rossi. She stared at his retreating back not knowing what to make of him. She'd seen the heat in his eyes when he looked at her body, but he hadn't tried anything. Instead, he seemed to be helping her. She wrinkled her brows in thought.

What game was he playing? She closed the shower door and leaned weakly against the wall while she tried to clear her head.

The way he had stared down at her body earlier left no doubt of his attraction to her. She let the steam from the shower seep into her, all while processing why he was there.

Admittedly, she had been avoiding him. She didn't like being manipulated and his play at negotiation still grated on her. A tiny voice at the back of her mind occasionally questioned whether she was avoiding him out of anger, or fear at her lack of control around him.

Her response to the whispered taunts was to place a mental ball gag on the voice and shove it back into the proverbial closet. Unfortunately, the little mental tart was well and truly free now and pestering at her. And the hussy no longer seemed content with sly whispers. Instead, all of the truths Veronica had avoided for weeks were hitting her in loud, full force.

Why hadn't she put up a fight? Why didn't she just get up and walk away? She had let Rossi finger-fuck her in a public place, for goodness' sake! She could have left at any moment, and despite his arrogance, she knew he wouldn't have forced her to stay.

No, she had stayed because she'd wanted to. She had wanted him to touch her. She still did, but she had needed an excuse, and pretending that she had no choice had been the easy scapegoat. Shaking her head, she reached for the soap and began to lather herself up.

It really didn't matter if she admitted that she wanted him. The man was still an arrogant ass who saw nothing wrong with manipulating people. Even if she was willing to forego her rule of not mixing business with pleasure, she wouldn't break it for him. No matter how tempted she was by him. She just had to convince her body of that, first.

Her hands began to tremble as she turned to rinse her body in the spray of water. Shudders began to wrack through her again despite the warmth of the shower. She was barely able to keep herself upright, let alone have a philosophical argument with herself.

She wearily scrubbed her hands over her face. She would just demand he tell her why he was there and she would ask him to leave so she could continue feeling like crap in peace. She could work on shoring up her defenses to him later. At the thought of the amount of effort that would take, she let out a small hysterical giggle.

"What's so funny?"

She heard Rossi's amused voice just moments before he opened the shower door. She couldn't muster the energy to try and cover herself. She could only look up at him with chattering teeth.

She took in his handsome grinning face and let her gaze roam down to his hard chest and to the still-bulging evidence at his crotch. She felt her heart sink, and held back a whimper as the ever-true phrase of *Resistance is futile* skittered through her mind.

"Is the concept of privacy beyond your comprehension?" she asked him irritably.

The bastard didn't even have the grace to look apologetic. He just shook his head, wrapped her efficiently in a towel, and lifted her out of the shower.

"Where are you finding the energy to be so sour when you can barely stand up by yourself?" he asked as he placed her feet gently on the floor and began to briskly rub her skin dry with the towel.

"Yeah, well, I'm talented like that," she said, trying to muster up a sneer.

Unfortunately, the feel of his brisk rubbing movements had slowed into teasing strokes. And she'd never thought the rough fibers of terry cloth could feel so damn erotic until that moment.

Perfection. That was the only word Victor's lust-filled mind could conjure to describe Veronica's body. He had started off with good intentions. He really had, but the moment he'd opened the shower door and seen all of her juicy, creamy naked skin, he'd been a goner. Her chattering teeth had been the only thing to keep him from dragging her to the floor and exploring her lush body.

When he lifted her out of the shower, he had honestly meant to dry her off quickly and help her to the bedroom so that she could eat and rest. Unfortunately, the moment he stroked the towel across her breasts and her nipples pebbled in reaction, all of his good intentions flew out the door.

His earlier observation had been right. Her breasts were more than a handful, and her nipples were perfect complements to them. He slowed his brisk rubbing down to light strokes, wanting to see her nipples extend even further. His mouth watered when they puckered into tight points. He wondered how they would feel against his tongue and the roof of his mouth. He wanted to gorge himself on them. He wanted to suck them into his mouth and have her squirm underneath him. He wanted to bite them softly and hear her gasp out in pleasure. God, he wanted to fuck her senseless.

His brain clouded with images of her coming apart in his arms. He licked his lips and tilted his head forward. *Just one taste*, he thought. *Just one taste of her succulent tits...*

"Ah-choo!"

Veronica's sneeze rang out through the air, snapping him out of his daze. His gaze shot up to her face and he saw her sniffle. He felt like an ass.

Shaking his head, he resumed his brisk rub down. After a few tense moments, he lifted her and carried her over to the bed. He laid her down gently and helped her sit up with her back against the headboard. He even helped bring the comforter up to cover her up to her neck.

"Do you think you can handle some food?" he asked gruffly, staring down into her wide eyes.

"I think I hate you," she replied back in a shaky voice.

He threw his head back and barked out a rough laugh.

"Well, there goes your dessert." He turned to her dresser and picked up a tray of food he'd placed there earlier. "I found some ice cream in the back of your freezer and now I'm just going to keep it all for myself," he continued as he placed the tray on her lap.

He watched as she stared down at the tray and looked back up to scowl at him.

"I'm not hungry," she said.

"Yes, you are. You're just feeling too sick to tell. If you finish at least half of the soup, I'll stop pestering you," he promised.

100

That statement seemed to galvanize her into motion. He held back another laugh as he watched her eat. He knew she thought he'd meant that he would leave if she ate. The woman was just too damn cute. He watched her for a few more moments before turning and heading back to the kitchen.

Once in the kitchen, he began gathering the makings of an old home remedy his mother used make for him when he was young. He concentrated on the basic movements of the task to keep his mind from thinking about Veronica and her delectable body. He boiled some water in a kettle and rummaged around the kitchen cabinets. After the water was done boiling, he finished making his concoction and poured the excess water into a small mug. He grabbed a clean dish towel, then picked up both mugs and headed back to the bedroom.

When he reached the bed, he placed both mugs on the night table and walked into the bathroom to search for some aspirin. Returning to the bedroom, he glanced down at her. Her eyes were drooping and her hand trembled as she struggled to bring a spoonful of soup to her lips.

"It looks like you've had enough," he said.

He leaned over, took the spoon from her

hand, and lifted the tray from her lap. Her eyes lifted to his in triumph.

"Yeah, thanks for the help," she started. "I'm sure you can see yourself out," she continued with a small smile spreading across her lips.

"Not so fast, Princess." He smiled down at her. "You still need to take something for that fever."

"I already told you. I don't have a fever. It's just a cold," she said belligerently.

"Yeah, well, humor me then and take this," he said as he handed her the aspirin and home remedy.

He watched her face and saw as she weighed her options. Once again, she seemed to decide that relenting to his request would get rid of him faster; she placed the aspirin in her mouth and raised the mug to her lips.

"Be careful, it's hot," he warned.

He watched as she sipped the hot brew and surprise lit across her face.

"This is a hot toddy." She looked up at him quizzically. "My mom always makes these for me when I'm sick."

"My mom used to do the same when I was young," he said, pulling a chair towards the

102

side of the bed. "She used to use limoncello, but I figured some rum and lime would work out just as well."

He reached for the second mug and dish cloth. Victor poured some of the hot water on the cloth. Just enough to heat it and make it slightly damp. Then, he reached over and flipped the comforter up to reveal her feet. Letting the cloth cool for just a few more seconds, he took her feet and wrapped them snuggly in the cloth. He heard her slight moan and looked up to see her face.

"God, that feels *so* good," she moaned out.

He grinned at her as he began to rub her feet through the warm cloth.

"I take it back," she said. "You can stay. Whatever you do, don't stop doing that."

A long sigh escaped her.

He smiled and continued rubbing for a few more minutes before removing the cloth and adding more hot water. He placed the cloth down on the night table and reached for the now empty mug in Veronica's hand.

"Turn over," he instructed.

He saw her struggle with the demand for a moment before she nodded and rolled over to lie on her stomach.

He pulled the comforter down to expose her

back, then reached for the warm cloth and placed it gently on her skin. He chuckled when she groaned again.

"My nephew has a pretty weak constitution," he explained as he began to rub her muscles through the cloth. "He was born premature, and even though he's nine years old now, he still doesn't have the best immune system. We learned this trick to help relieve shivers and aching muscles a few years ago after he got a nasty flu bug. He's a good kid, but very stubborn. He hates getting sick, so he pretends like he's not hurting and that only makes it worse," he added as he worked his hands down her back.

"It sounds like you love him a lot," Veronica said, her voice coming out in a soft whisper.

Victor chuckled as he thought of his precocious nephew. "Yeah, his name is David, and he's probably the most amazing kid in the world. His dad died a few years ago and he considers himself the man of the house. He told me the other day to start calling him Mr. David," he said, shaking his head.

He felt her shoulders move as she

laughed softly.

"He sounds like a handful," she said drowsily.

"He is, but I wouldn't change him for anything."

He told her stories about his nephew as he continued to rub at her sore muscles. She asked a few more questions, but after a while, she drifted into silence. Eventually, he heard her release a soft snore, and smiled. She was asleep. He removed the cloth from her skin, rolled her onto her back, and pulled the comforter back up to her neck before her body could tempt him into doing something stupid.

He glanced down at his watch and wasn't surprised to see that it was only seven in the evening. *Thank God for smart phones,* he thought as he left the room and settled onto her couch. He figured he could get some work in and still be around if she needed him.

CHAPTER ELEVEN

Veronica shuddered awake and, for a moment, thought she was back in New York. She was freezing, and it took her a second to realize she hadn't woken up in a cold, unheated apartment; she was sick and it felt horrible. She curled into herself, shivering so hard her teeth rattled.

Her body ached and she felt frozen to the core. She hated being sick. The helplessness of it always made her want to scream out in frustration. She burrowed further into the blankets and tried to fight back tears.

Mother Nature was always the great equalizer, she thought. No matter how capable and strong you thought you were, Nature would bitch-slap you with some virus, germ, or otherwise generally hellacious ailment that had even the strongest person whimpering for their momma. She had definitely reached that point.

She wished she hadn't made Victor leave. As

obnoxious as he was, it did suck to be sick and alone. Tears fell down her cheeks unchecked and she just hoped sleep would envelop her again.

"Hey, you're awake."

The sound his gruff voice almost made her sob out in relief.

"You're still here," she whispered.

"Of course, I am. I told you it was going to take a lot to make me leave," he said as he leaned over her and touched his hand to her brow. "You're still really hot."

"I don't feel hot," she said. "I feel like someone dumped a pile of ice on top of me."

"Well, to sound completely cliché, I know how to warm you up. He waggled his eyebrows at her and twisted his mouth into a comical leer.

"You're a pervert," she said with a small, tired smile stretching her lips.

"You can't blame a man for trying," he said, returning her smile.

"Like I said, pervert."

"Well, this pervert is going to get you some more aspirin and see about turning on some heat," he said as he turned and left the room.

Watching him walk away, a strange

thought flickered through her mind. That even an arrogant, manipulative, pervert could be the sweetest nursemaid.

When he returned with the aspirin, she still had a smile on her face.

"Unfortunately, your a/c doesn't have a heating option, so the best I could do was to just turn it off, so at least you're not getting a draft of cool air," he said as he helped her sit up in the bed.

Testing his resolve, Veronica let the blanket slip slightly to expose the upper swell of her breasts. She hid her smirk behind the mug he hastily handed her along with some aspirin.

"Thanks," she said and handed him back the mug. "What time is it?"

She didn't know how long she'd slept, and she found the idea of Victor roaming around her apartment for hours a little jarring.

"It's just past two a.m."

"Are you serious? I can't believe you've stayed here all this time."

He just shrugged his shoulders and joined her on the bed. He swung his feet up on the mattress and leaned his head against the headboard. He crossed his arms across his chest and yawned loudly.

"It's no big deal. I got some work done,

channel surfed, ate all of your Rocky Road, and fell asleep on your couch."

"You're lucky I'm so weak, or you'd be maimed by now. I take my ice cream very seriously," she said, sending him a mock scowl.

"I'll count myself blessed, then," he replied drowsily. He reached an arm over her shoulders and dragged her close to his chest. "Get some sleep; you'll feel better in the morning," he said as he rested his chin on top of her heard.

She heard him release another loud yawn. He felt so solid and warm she was reluctant to move. She knew she should tell him to go home and get some rest of his own, but she wanted to feel his warmth just a little while longer. After a few minutes, she heard him release a muffled snore, and she smiled, snuggling into him more. There was no harm in letting him get a few more minutes' sleep, she thought as her eyes drifted closed.

Victor drifted awake slowly, not wanting to leave the depths of the best sleep he'd had in ages. He was on the verge of falling back into slumber when his senses gradually registered the feel of soft skin beneath his palms and a warm body curled into his. He inhaled deeply, and the heady scent of honey and coconut filled his senses. *Veronica.*

He opened his eyes and felt a moment of complete contentment. Veronica slept facing him and curled up into his chest. Her hands were fisted in his shirt and her face was relaxed in sleep, with her soft lips slightly parted. The sight made him sigh in pleasure.

He lifted a hand to her smooth face. It felt cool against his palm. Her fever had finally broken. He smiled slightly when he recalled how irritable she was yesterday. Staring down into her face, he felt a puzzle piece fall into place.

Veronica wasn't just a woman he wanted to spend time with. She wasn't just a woman that enticed him and filled him with lust. She wasn't just a woman he wanted to call his. She was *the* woman. The woman he spent years avoiding and running from. The woman he would fall in love with. If he was completely honest with himself, he was already more than halfway there. He already felt his heart tightening at the thought of her not wanting him.

No wonder love drives people crazy, he thought. The feelings that were rumbling through his mind and heart had driven him to desperate measures with her. They were what drove him to propose this outrageous contract.

Looking back now, he could see it had been a mistake.

Veronica was a strong woman and contrary as hell. He should have known that the way to win her was not to back her into a corner. Her stubborn nature pretty much guaranteed him a fight. He knew she felt the same attraction he did, but as for any deeper feelings, his current method of pursuit would not be able to unearth.

He was going to have to change tactics.

If he wanted a real relationship with her, he would have to let her come to him out of her own need to be with him. He tightened his arms around her and breathed in her scent one more time before slowly disentangling his body from hers. He refused to believe that his feelings were one-sided.

He walked out of the bedroom with firm resolve. He paused in the living room and scrawled a succinct note.

Victor returned to the bedroom and left the note on his abandoned pillow. He stared down into her sleeping face one last time before turning to leave her apartment, hoping with every step that he was making the right decision.

CHAPTER TWELVE

Veronica fought against a pressing sense of *déjà vu*. She was sitting in Victor's waiting room at Niles Enterprises once again waiting for the always-running-late CEO to appear for a meeting. For once, she wasn't alone.

The four VPs of the company, along with its junior group of programmers, sat along with her. The group had assembled for the final presentation to the board and CLEO's official launch. Unlike all of the other times she sat waiting for Victor, she felt an odd sense of calm.

Ever since he'd left his note for her last week, she had been waiting for the moment when she would be face to face with him again.

She had woken up that morning to find his brief letter on her pillow. In one short note, he had turned her world upside down.

Veronica,

Our contract arrangement is now null and void. Consider the playing field even. Your retainer contract is still valid and expected to be maintained.
~Victor

She shook her head as she recited the letter cynically in her head. With three short sentences, he had thrown the ball completely into her court, and she was forced to face some very annoying truths. The first being that she was more than a little sad to not have woken in his arms that morning. The second, and even more difficult to admit—she didn't just want Victor in a physical sense. She wanted him because she felt an emotional draw to him that she knew warranted more than just a brief sexual encounter. The third and worst truth was the knowledge that she had been running from that emotional draw like a big, fat baby for weeks.

She had used her rule of not mixing business with pleasure as a shield to prevent her from acknowledging her real feelings. She was even grown enough to admit that she always had. For years, she had preferred casual relationships that provided physical satisfaction and basic comfort over anything deeper.

She hadn't wanted anything to interfere with her drive for success, and she had to admit she had never met a man worth breaking any rules for. Until Victor. Unfortunately, instead of taking a chance, she had held stubbornly to the idea that her attraction was purely physical and could be tamped down. All she had to show for her stubbornness was loneliness and what felt suspiciously like a bruised heart.

Thankfully, as her college GPA could attest to, she was no fool. After moping around her apartment for the better part of two days, she finally came up with what she thought as the perfect solution to her problem. She was going to get her man in the only way that gave them both the advantage.

She smiled to herself and looked down at the pile of presentation folios in her lap. She couldn't wait to begin the negotiations.

"Mr. Rossi is ready to see you all," Marie said in her soft, calm voice.

Veronica took a deep breath and stood with the rest of the group. As she walked sedately into his office, she couldn't keep a small smile of anticipation from spreading across her face.

Victor watched as Veronica made her way into his office. He gave brief greetings to the rest of the group, but could not keep his eyes off her. She wore the same sexy suit she had worn several weeks ago when he had made his panty proposition to her. He drank in the sight of her. He had missed her.

The past few days had been difficult. He'd reconsidered his decision to let her come to him about a million times a day. Just that morning, he had woken from yet another heated dream of her, and he was quickly reaching his breaking point.

If she didn't give him any indication of softening her stance soon, he would have to come up with a new game plan.

Just being in the same room with her again had his skin tightening and his dick stirring to life.

Veronica spared him only a brief glance and a smooth "Good Morning" before turning to the large monitor set up in front of his conference table.

He fought back a frown as he exchanged brief pleasantries with the rest of the group while they all gathered around the gleaming marble surface and took their seats.

He took his place at the head of the long

table and spoke across to her.

"We're ready when you are, Ms. James. We're all eager to see the final product."

"I think you'll be more than satisfied with the end result," she said, smiling to the group at large, her gaze touching on each person and making contact.

When her eyes met his, he thought he saw them soften somewhat, but she quickly glanced away.

"We've incorporated all of your must-have requirements and most of the items on your wish list, so let's get started," she said.

Victor nodded at her statement. She picked up a stack of presentation folios and reached over to press the switch to dim the lights.

The overhead lights dimmed completely and small, individual reading lamps switched on the table with soft focus. Each bulb cast a small, diffuse light in front of every person, providing just enough clarity to view the papers in front of them.

Veronica began to walk around the table, placing a blue folio in front of each person seated as she passed by.

"Along with today's presentation, I've put together some metrics from the feedback we received from the pilot testing group along with suggestions for some possible expansions for the future," she said.

When she reached his side, she placed a red folio in front of him. Victor noticed the difference from the other folios in the group. He raised his gaze and gave her a questioning look. She smiled and leaned towards him slightly.

"I've included some additional in-depth analysis for you to review," she said softly before straightening and continuing around the rest of the table.

He opened the folio, flipped through the first few pages, and nodded his head in understanding. He wasn't surprised that she'd gone above and beyond, as usual. She really was damn good at what she did.

He watched as she made her way back around to the end of the table and lifted a small remote into her hand. She pointed the device towards the large monitor, and the first image of CLEO flickered then sharpened into clarity on the screen.

"Ladies and gentlemen, we present to you CLEO," she said proudly with a wide smile spreading across her lips.

A short round of applause followed her statement, and there was no denying her pride in the project.

She began pointing out different features of the finished application. As she spoke, he couldn't help but feeling a swell of pride for her himself. She had worked hard on the software, and she spoke so smoothly and confidently that a person couldn't help but be caught up in her excitement.

"This is a big improvement over the original, barebones application," she stated.

He noticed her falter slightly before continuing.

"If you turn to page six of your folios, you'll see comparison metrics of this new version versus the original."

She paused briefly as everyone around the table began flipping through their folios.

She stared pointedly at him and he gave himself a mental shake. He had been so wrapped up in watching her that he hadn't wanted to take his eyes away from her.

He looked down at his own report and began to flip through the pages. When he reached the sixth page, his breath caught in his throat.

Sweet Jesus, he thought before lifting the folio and tilting it in towards his chest, effectively blocking anyone's view of the page.

His gaze quickly scanned the other folios

around the table. Nothing seemed unusual and no one else seemed surprised in any way.

He stared back at his folio and gulped in a mouthful of air. On his page, surrounded by innocuous technical jargon and charts, was an image of a decidedly more graphic nature.

One of Veronica dressed exactly as she was at that moment, but with several important exceptions. The image showed her facing away from the camera. She was slightly bent forward with her skirt raised up around her hips. Her fingers were hooked into her thong, which was dragged down just past the juncture of her thighs, giving him a perfect view of her luscious ass and pussy from behind.

Sweat broke across his forehead as he struggled to breathe. He was amazed no one heard the sound of his dick smacking the zipper of his pants. The image in front of him had him hard as a spike in seconds.

"Is there a problem, Mr. Rossi?" Veronica's husky voice came from across the room.

Victor raised his heated gaze to meet hers. She quirked an eyebrow at him as a small flirty smile played across her lips.

"Your report has additional details that might be better discussed at the end of this presentation. We can explore the details further then, perhaps," she said.

He had to clear his voice before responding. Trust her to come up with the most frustrating way possible to wave a white flag of surrender. He didn't think his dick would survive the next hour.

"Of course," he managed to reply smoothly before he ran a trembling hand through his hair.

"Perfect. Let's continue, shall we?" she said to the group around the table. "CLEO is now completely web-based. Employees can access it through multiple internet browsers. On page eight, you'll see the complete browser compatibility list highlighting the enhanced ease of access."

Victor began to flip through his report again, but a strange sense of intuition stopped him before turning over to the noted page. He glanced up to look at her, and saw a wicked smile play across her lips. He looked back down and took a deep breath to brace himself before turning the page.

She's trying to kill me, he thought

desperately a second later as he stared down at the image on the page. This one showed her spread-eagle on her bed, her pussy bared naked, open, and wet, to the camera.

He struggled to keep his breath even and smooth despite his racing heart. The woman was playing with fire, and damn if he didn't love her for it.

He shifted slightly in his chair, trying to relieve the pressure of his aching dick. He looked back up and saw heat flare in her gaze before she turned back to the screen and continued with the presentation.

The minutes ticked by slowly for him. His skin was tight with restraint and all he could think about was dragging her across the conference table and fucking her senseless. His brain just couldn't think beyond the image of her cunt open and wet for him.

This was the invitation he had been waiting for, and the contrary woman had issued it as both an invite and a challenge. Each ticking second was a battle of wills between them. She knew what she had done to him and was enjoying the struggle.

A part of him welcomed the challenge and loved the anticipation. Veronica was his match in every way.

As the end of the hour slowly approached, Victor grew convinced that she was deliberately drawing out the presentation. He shifted several times in frustration and, with each shift, she sent him a naughty little smile. Despite her discrete flirtatious looks, he was able to keep himself in check...just barely. His heart was no longer racing but his dick was still hard enough to fuck a hole through the marble-topped table.

"The final point I'd like to address is staff training," she finally said. "As you can see, CLEO is now a fully-functional application. But unfortunately, some employees may find the transition difficult."

She pointed the remote to the screen and threw a glance over her shoulder. The smile that spread across her lips had his heart speeding up again in earnest.

"If you'll turn to page twenty-six, you'll see the staff training projections," she said.

He almost didn't want to look, but the heat and challenge in her gaze had him looking down and turning to the page.

Fuck Me. His hands clenched into fists as he looked down at the final image on the page. It showed Veronica lying with her legs spread, knees bent, and feet planted firmly on her bed. She held a large dildo in her hand, pushing the bulbous tip of the tool into her dripping flesh. The image was deliciously raunchy, but what had his heart stopping were the words written boldly along the length of the fake cock.

Fuck Me.

"As you can see, with proper motivation and encouragement from upper management, there should be no problem with having the entire staff fully trained in a minimum amount of time."

Veronica pressed the switch to turn the overhead lights back on, and a loud round of applause came from around the table.

Victor let his gaze travel down her body. Her skin glowed and her breathing was slightly labored.

Anyone looking at her would assume those things were just a sign of her excitement over the demonstration, but his gaze didn't miss the evidence of her stiffened nipples or trembling hands by her side.

She just stood there staring at him, her wet, pink tongue darting out to lick her lips, promising him heaven and hell all in one swipe.

His control snapped.

"Thank you, Ms. James," he said, not trying to hide the gruffness of his voice. "If you all would excuse us, I'd like to discuss the additional details of my report now."

His tone left no room for argument, and the group of VPs and programmers hurried out of the office, oblivious to the smoldering fog of anticipation in the air.

He didn't let his gaze waver from hers. When the door closed behind the final person, he pressed the intercom unit at the table and spoke softly to his assistant. "Marie, cancel all remaining appointments for the afternoon and go ahead and leave early."

"Yes, sir," the efficient voice replied through the speaker.

He watched as Veronica sat calmly down in a chair at the end of the table and crossed her legs. She quirked an eyebrow at him and her message was clear. *Come and get me.*

His dick hardened further in response to her brazen provocation.

He stood and began stalking towards her. He shrugged off his suit jacket not bothering to see where it landed.

"Just so we're clear," he said as he removed his tie and threw it over his shoulder.

He reached over and swiveled her chair around towards him, placing his hands on the armrests and effectively caging her in. He leaned forward, his nostrils flaring at the scent of her. She wasn't as unaffected as she pretended to be. He could smell her arousal. The scent was like a wet, heavy cloak surrounding her.

He gave her his own wicked smile as that small victory whipped through his system.

"That," he said, motioning towards his abandoned folio at the head of the table, "is considered an invitation."

She tilted her head back and brought her plush mouth so close to his that her lips brushed his when she spoke softly.

"Just so we're clear," she replied huskily, "it is."

He gave a rumbling sound of satisfaction before clamping his lips on hers in a hungry kiss.

CHAPTER | THIRTEEN

Veronica's body sang out in relief at the feel of his mouth claiming hers. His kiss was a commanding tangle of nipping teeth and thrusting tongue and she wanted to drown in it.

The taste of him exploded across her senses, mingling with the already heady scents of his heated skin and spicy cologne.

She needed to get closer to him, needed to feel all of his heat against her body. She surged to the edge of her chair and hooked her arms around his neck, trying to pull him closer. As if sensing her frustration, he stood, dragging her along with him. She sighed in relief at the first feel of his chest pressed against hers.

He snaked his palms down to her ass and slammed her pelvis into him. The feel of his cock hard and throbbing against her stomach pulled a moan from her throat. God, he felt so good, so damn right against her. She could barely think. All she could do was rub against him, trying to get closer.

She hadn't expected her plan to be so double-edged. She'd meant it to be an invitation and a challenge. She'd wanted him to know she was willing to share the control so that they could both be satisfied. He got to chase and she got to be captured, but she hadn't expected this gnawing need.

Her womb was clenching and her breasts were heavy and tight with want.

Watching his reactions to her pictures had turned her on to an explosive degree. Each shift of his body and heated gaze had licked a wave of heat through her.

The need to stretch his breaking point had warred with her need to prolong her own anticipation and aching arousal.

He grabbed her thigh and raised her knee up to his side. His hands found the edge of her skirt and shoved it up to her waist. She could only groan her agreement and hooked her leg around his waist, pulling him in closer.

His answering grunt turned into a moan as his hands found her bare flesh and ground her against him. It wasn't enough. She needed more.

Her pussy had long passed *drenched*, and her clit was throbbing a tattooed rhythm that had her desperate to have him inside her, desperate to feel his throbbing heat thrusting into her.

She whimpered a protest when his mouth left hers.

"No," she whispered, desperately pulling his head back down to hers.

He jerked his head back. His teeth were clenched and his breaths came out in quick pants. He shook his head as if to clear it. His palms clenched on her ass cheeks before pulling her away from him.

"Naked, now," he demanded as he began shoving his shirt from his chest.

Yes, naked, she thought. She needed see all of him.

The hard expanse of his chest was just as delicious as she imagined—a hard, bronzed landscape of muscle and sinew. Her mouth watered at the thought of running her lips over the curves of his pecs and the rigid planes of his stomach.

She licked her lips as he worked his belt free of his pants. Since the day she'd caught him masturbating, she had fantasized about his dick. She wanted to fill her mouth with it, to taste him as he exploded down her throat.

His hands stilled at his zipper, and her gaze flew up to his face in desperate question.

"I said *now*," he barked as he lunged forward. He clasped the edges of her blouse and ripped it open.

Buttons scattered into the air and clanged to the floor. She was barely able to get out a gasp before he pulled her back in for a scorching kiss.

She reached up with her hands to stroke across his chest to his naked back. She tried to pull him closer but his hands kept her back as he removed the rest of her clothing. When he finally stopped blocking her movements, she pressed herself against him and they both moaned at the feel of her naked breasts caressed against his chest.

Yes, this was much better, this skin-to-skin merging. Why she had fought so hard against this perfection was beyond her comprehension.

He lifted her up and she wrapped her legs around his waist. She felt his stomach clench at the feel of her moist center rubbing against it.

He leaned forward and she felt the cool

touch of the hard granite conference table on her bottom.

She felt his hands blaze a path up her ribs and cup her breasts. He cradled her breasts in his hands, palming them before squeezing roughly. She squirmed on the table, her body begging for his possessive touch.

His fingers swept forward and he began tugging at her nipples, pulling them forward in short pinches. He pulled his mouth away from her lips and trailed hot kisses down her throat, licking and nipping at her skin in hunger.

When his wet mouth finally wrapped around a taut nipple, she couldn't hold back her loud groan.

He grunted in response, raising his lips only long enough to push the two aching globes together. Her nipples scraped against each other and he hissed his approval at the sight before taking them both into his mouth.

He tongued and sucked at her nipples until she was drowning in the need for release. She arched her back, surrendering her body to him.

Her legs pulled tight at his back as she ground herself against him. Her slick folds rubbed against the ridges of his stomach and she knew she was close to exploding. She was so close to release she could feel the prickly heat of it scorch down her spine.

Just as that realization came to her, she felt his hands leave her breasts and his lips released her nipples. She sobbed out a protest and tried to pull his mouth back to them. He couldn't stop; she was so close.

He grabbed her hands and slammed them down to her sides on the table. She arched against him as his lips trailed down her stomach. He twirled his hot tongue around her navel before traveling down her pelvis and settling at the top of her mons.

She stilled completely, her body wound tight with the need to feel his hot tongue lick into her center.

Victor did not disappoint. He slicked his tongue down through her folds. The tip burned over her throbbing clit and pressed hard before moving down. As he curled his tongue into her clenching pussy for his first deep taste, her control finally snapped and she came in a fiery rush of pleasure.

Victor had never felt so out of control. His only thought was to devour Veronica, his only goal to gorge himself on her. He released her hands and grabbed her thighs.

He dropped to his knees as he spread her wide open. The taste and smell of her release filled his senses.

He stroked his hands up and spread her pussy wide. He pulled his face back to stare at it in awe. Her cunt was plump and juicy with arousal, and her slit, still clenching in the aftershocks of her first release, dripped with cream. The sight had him groaning and lunging forward for another taste.

He needed to feel her come underneath his mouth one more time. He needed to see those luscious lips puffy and swollen and hear her scream out in release again.

He plunged his tongue into her and felt her walls clench around it. She was absolute perfection. He heard her whimper softly and he felt her hands scrape through the hair at the nape of his neck and pull him forward.

She ground herself against his mouth as he plunged his tongue into her hungrily over and over again.

Her hips began to move in frenzied jerks and he replaced his tongue with two fingers, penetrating her hard and fast as he licked up to her clit. He felt her thighs clamp tightly around his head and her whole body began to quiver hotly underneath his mouth.

Laurel Cremant

Her curled his fingers up into her slit and wrapped his lips around her beautifully engorged clit, sucking it into his mouth. Her pussy clamped down hard on his fingers as she came again.

He could only groan in hunger at the sound of her shouting out her release. He gave her pussy one last swipe before surging to his feet. He needed to get inside her now.

He stared down at her laid out on the table. Her body was on decadent display. Her breasts were swollen and her nipples were tightly erect. Her legs were hanging over the edge and her thighs were spread wide, presenting her pussy glistening from his mouth and her release.

She was fucking beautiful.

She stirred and sinuously sat up, placing her hands flat on the table behind her. The position spread her legs wider and arched her breasts high. Her drowsy eyes lifted to his as she whispered his name.

The sound of her voice husky with need broke his last link of control.

He ripped at the zipper of his pants and released his aching dick from its confines. It was already slick with pre-cum, ready to sink into her. He yanked his wallet from his

136

back pocket, quickly removing a condom, and rolling it down his length.

Their gazes locked as he stepped between her thighs and pulled her ass to the edge of the table, tilting her pussy to the perfect angle for fucking.

He guided his dick to her center and let it slip between her folds. They both sucked in a breath as heat met heat. He rubbed the head of his cock around her clit, torturing them both, before placing his cock at the mouth of her pussy.

He was desperate to plunge into her. Desperate to feel her wet, clinging heat clench around him, but he needed one more surrender, one more term negotiated.

"We're going on a date," he said around clenched teeth.

He saw her eyes open wide in surprise.

"I don't care where, I don't care what, but we're going to go out and do date-like things. I'm going to learn your favorite color and you're going to learn mine," he ordered, his voice coming out in harsh pants.

Joy and relief coursed through him as he saw a wide smile spread across her face.

"I want to go to the movies for our first date. We can negotiate the locations of all future dates, and my favorite color is green," she said huskily.

He groaned as he plunged into her balls-deep. Her cunt was tight and hot around him. She fell back on the table at the force of his thrust, but he couldn't stop himself from surging forward again and again. He clenched his hands on her ass as he pounded into her.

She lifted her legs and wrapped them around his waist, holding him tight.

He watched as she smoothed her hands up her torso and cupped her breasts, offering them to him. He moaned as he leaned over and sucked a proffered nipple into his mouth while he plunged in and out of her wet heat.

Heat seared from his neck, traveling down his spine, and pooling around his crotch. He wanted to sink into her forever. He could feel her juices dripping down his balls and the thought of having her cum all over him took him to the edge of climax. He snaked a hand between their bodies to finger her clit.

Her cunt swelled and tightened further around him. She was moaning and writhing beneath him, but it wasn't enough. He needed to feel her gush all around him, needed to feel her pussy fist tight on his hard flesh.

He bit down lightly on her nipple and pinched her swollen clit. He heard her gasp out his name just before her pussy clamped down hard around him. He felt her pussy shivering around his length, massaging it, milking him as her release dripped down his cock.

He roared out his release, his dick jerking deep inside of her. His body shook with the force of his release. He slumped forward, his body crushing hers to the table, and felt her arms reach up and hold him tight to her.

After a few minutes of dazed and labored breathing, he leaned up onto his forearms and looked down into her face.

She smiled up at him as she hooked her hands behind his head.

"Just so you know, I'm not usually such an easy date. I think we might have to negotiate the terms of our next sexual encounter. I don't want you thinking this relationship is only about sex," she said coyly.

His dick twitched and hardened to life inside her. She gasped out in surprise before a wicked smile tilted her lips up in provocation and invitation.

The woman loved to throw down a challenge,

and he planned on spending the rest of his life rising to them.

"I think I can come up with a few persuasive arguments," he said before swooping his mouth down for a long kiss.

THE END

Turn the page for a sneak peek of the contemporary romance, **RAPT** *by Laurel Cremant.*

Chapter One

"*Will you walk into my parlour?*" *said the Spider to the fly.*

Lucas Wright smiled as he thought of the line from an old children's fable. He'd never considered himself a predator, but the ever-pressing need to devour one Ms. Jessica Wright convinced him otherwise. For almost a year, he had wanted nothing more than to drag her to his bed and wrap her in so much pleasure she'd never leave.

He shook his head derisively as he stood up from his workout mat. Sweat dripped down his bare chest and abdomen. Even after almost two exhausting hours of intense yoga, his muscles tightened and his cock stirred to attention at the image of her forming in his mind, all bothered and wet, stretched out on his bed.

Soon.

Today, he planned to take action.

He walked to edge of his hotel suite and stepped out onto the large glass rimmed balcony. Pulling in a deep breath, he let the warm salty breeze of the Fort Lauderdale coastline fill his lungs and calm his building anticipation. By tonight, he would know for sure whether Jessica was willing to take their flirtations to another level.

If she's honest with herself.

And that was the crux of it. He wondered if she was ready to admit that they'd both been playing a long drawn out game for quite some time. Each of them pushing the boundaries of their professional relationship and testing the waters. For months, they had danced around each other, whether Jessica chose to admit it or not. In the beginning, he'd almost missed it. Caught up in his own need to control his attraction and baser instincts he'd almost missed the signs.

Lucas hired her to be his chief acquisitions actuary. His company specialized in mergers and acquisitions. When his previous actuary retired, Jessica had come highly recommended. Upon reviewing her resume, he noted she was bright, driven, and after

144

interviewing her for over an hour, he'd added tenacious and perfect for the job to her list of qualifications.

However, from the moment Jessica stepped into his office he'd wanted her for more than just her skills in the field. She'd reminded him of a painting he purchased several years before. Titled Calypso, the picture depicted a curvaceous, naked black woman sprawled on a throne, her head turned as she stared out at the ocean. One leg dangled over the side of the chair while the other trailed on the floor, her feet pointed and delicate looking. The painting had hit him like a punch to the gut and he'd purchased it on the spot. The first time he met Jessica he had the same reaction.

He'd been instantly attracted by the soft lush curves hugged underneath her deep gray pencil skirt. The full pout of her full lips as she spoke to him in a soft husky voice had him aroused in seconds and the creamy smoothness of her chocolate skin had him itching to reach out and test its softness. Every inch of her seemed designed to entice him—from her warm brown eyes, down her luscious body, to the point of her stiletto-heeled shoes. She exuded a combination of confidence and intelligence that only added to her allure. However, at the age of thirty-eight, he'd learned enough in his lifetime to not to let attraction get in the way of business.

He had a hard and staunch rule of never mixing business with pleasure. Aside from it just being a sound business practice, his rule allowed him to maintain a certain level of privacy. One of the pitfalls of owning a company as large as his was that people became inordinately interested in his personal life. Since he had no intention of handing over his business or going broke anytime soon—it was drawback to success he accepted whole-heartedly.

His sexual preferences were also a part of his need for privacy. Although he didn't fully immerse himself into the world of BDSM, he'd learned a long time ago that he was a moderate sexual sadist. Unlike most people, his revelation didn't come as an epiphany or gradual understanding of his psyche. Growing up with two college professors as parents he was surrounded by scientific and medical journals his entire life. By the time he had his first sexual experience, he'd recognized and accepted his sexuality. He'd even had a few rather frank discussions with his parents regarding the matter. Being the child of two very progressive, former hippie parents had its advantages.

However, embracing his sexuality didn't mean he wanted it open to public discussion. He was very selective in choosing lovers. Although he didn't find it difficult to find women willing to dabble in his lifestyle, over the last few years he wanted more and more a woman willing to play long-term.

The clock is ticking.

He smiled derisively at that thought. Lately he'd felt as if time was ticking by too quickly. He'd grown up an only child and had always wanted a large family. Although he wanted a woman willing to submit her pleasure to him in bed, he also wanted a strong female role model for his future children. He looked back on the long drawn out discussions his parents would have at the dinner table with fondness. They discussed everything from movies to global geopolitics with passion and he wanted that same type of relationship with the woman he chose to marry. Finding that woman seemed easier said than done—until he'd met Jessica.

Jessica had surprised him. Not only did he find the tall, dark beauty sexy, he appreciated her keen intelligence and sharp wit. Every now and then he would sense vulnerability in her, but her take charge, no-nonsense personality masked any softness well. That combination of hard and soft intrigued him and had the sadist and him, among other things, standing at attention.

She personified the type of woman he wanted to pursue and so much more. It took him a while to admit that he'd fallen for her but something about her tugged at him, making it difficult for him to ignore. His stance of not mixing business with pleasure had been the only thing holding him back. However, all that changed when he realized, Jessica was fighting the same attraction. Not only that—she also seemed to enjoy the mounting sexual tension as much as he did. It seemed his sexy actuary exhibited a touch of sexual masochism.

It started small. He'd notice her long glances down his body when she thought no one was looking, her hitched breathing as their meetings progressed—the hard pebbling of her nipples beneath her blouse. He'd recognized those signs.

When he first began exploring the BDSM lifestyle, he'd encountered more than a few masochists who enjoyed prolonging sexual stimulation. One woman in particular enjoyed masturbating for days prior to seeking any relief. He could see her glassy eyed arousal mirrored in Jessica's behavior as the months progressed.

He began anticipating each meeting with her. Testing her limits by prolonging their discussions and watching her body tighten and squirm with each passing minute. The air hung heavy with the scent of her arousal—the ultimate aphrodisiac. He'd inhaled the scent his mouth watering at the implication. He marveled that she thought he wouldn't notice how aroused she was as she sat in front of him, crossing and uncrossing her legs every few minutes. He dragged that meeting out—the sadist in him couldn't help it—and watched as her breath caught repeatedly.

When he finally decided to end the meeting, she stood on shaky legs as he escorted her out of the office. Even after tormenting her for so long he couldn't resist the urge to confirm his suspicions. As he'd reached to open the door, he deliberately grazed his arm against the front of her blouse, sweeping across her hard nipples. Her slick lips fell open on a gasp, and her eyes had blazed with an almost crazed passion.

He let her escape that day with a murmured apology, he'd watched her stumble down the hall to her office and slam the door shut—his lips curling up in a wide grin.

There was nothing a sadist liked better than a game of denial and patience.

He'd been playing the same game ever since. Knowing she was aroused, prolonging meetings to see just how long she could last. Their meetings were becoming an addiction for him and fantasizing about what she did each time she left him kept his body on overdrive and caused more than a few sleepless nights.

Not many women were into his preferred method of sexual dominance. His brand of sadism focused almost exclusively on sexual denial—on having a woman submit control to him and allowing him to decide when they would receive pleasure. The slow delay or denial of pleasure and gradual buildup of arousal gave him the power to deconstruct a person's orgasm. That type of power dynamic and play turned him on like nothing else. Finding a partner to indulge with proved more difficult than most people would think.

Most women loved the concept of extended foreplay, but when he prolonged it passed an hour or more without allowing them to come, they weren't exactly happy to meet his acquaintance.

Leaning his elbows on the railing, he stared out over the small crowd of sunbathers and tourists below on the beach, his gaze resting the perfect cerulean blue of the ocean beyond.

Lucas recalled the brief emails she'd exchanged with him that day and released a short breath. Her current assignment was over and as usual, she would make her way to him to deliver her final report and analysis in person. In a little over an hour Jessica would arrive and the anticipation of it was already tightening his skin and heating his blood. To tell the truth he'd been running on high since the moment she'd messaged him earlier in the day. He'd prolonged his yoga routine in the hopes of exhausting his body and diminishing his libido.

No such luck.

He should have known better. Pushing back from the rail, he turned and walked back into his suite and stretched his arms over head, trying to release the mounting tension spreading across his shoulders. Dropping his hands down to his waist he untied his drawstring pants and let them fall to the floor before making his way into the bathroom. He stepped into the cool marble shower enclosure and locked his knees tight before twisting on the water.

He whispered a soft curse as cold water

sluiced down his body. As the freezing water beat down on his skin, Lucas consoled himself with a single thought. Tonight he would either find relief or learn definitively that Jessica was hands off.

* * *

The office smelled like sex—again.

Jessica Wright cut her gaze to the flustered woman holding the door open for her. The woman's lips were swollen and bare of lipstick while her high cheekbones were tinged a bright hue of red. All of that, combined with the woman's mussed hair and rumpled clothing, left Jessica with no doubt that the woman and the man sitting smugly at his desk had just engaged in some extracurricular office activity.

I don't get paid enough for this.

Releasing her breath in a quick huff, Jessica stepped over the threshold into the sleek office of Shepard Electronics CEO, Richard Planks. The door closed with a soft snick behind her. Despite her disgust for Planks, she couldn't keep her pulse from speeding up in anticipation. Not for her meeting with Planks but for what would happen afterward. Dealing with Planks now meant she would see Lucas Wright later.

Lucas Wright. Her current employer and guilty pleasure. Because of him her usual enjoyment of dealing with scum like Planks was heightened with the knowledge that seeing Wright always followed. Tingling pinpricks raced across her skin and her palms began to sweat. Suppressing the need to rub them down the sides of her skirt she kept her gaze trained on Planks.

"I hope I didn't interrupt anything important," she said as she walked towards him.

"Nothing that couldn't be rescheduled," he replied in the low nasal drawl indicative of his Bostonian roots.

Oh, I'm sure.

He didn't rise from his seat as she entered the room. Not that she expected him to. The man was sleazy arrogance personified. He'd made it clear since she first arrived several weeks ago, that he wasn't worried about what her investigation might find. That didn't surprise her. In her line of work, she'd found that regardless of level of wealth—greed and hubris were equal opportunity vices amongst people in powerful positions.

Richard Planks indulged in both to the point of addiction.

He sat at his desk, his tailored suite rumpled, a satisfied smile twitching at his lips. She wondered for the hundredth time, how a man so stupid managed to become CEO of such a large corporation. She'd perused thousands of financial data proving her assessment. Richard Planks wasn't only a sleaze—he was also a thief and a cheat. And the man truly believed his machinations wouldn't be discovered.

Fool.

She didn't wait for permission to be seated. Planks wasn't the type to extend an invitation. He liked people to feel uncomfortable around him. Jessica had no patience for his silly power play. Sitting down, she leaned back into the soft leather chair and crossed her legs. She watched as his gaze followed the movement of her legs, lingering for a moment on the small stretch of thigh revealed by the hem of her skirt. The leer curling across his features didn't bother her. It only served to make the moment to come so much sweeter.

Her lips trembled as she tried to keep a wide smile from stretching across her mouth. This was the part of her job she loved the most—the moment when smug men like Planks were gob-smacked with truth.

She'd spent years studying and training to

become an actuary and for the last year she'd had the exclusive pleasure of being Lucas Wright's acquisitions actuary. Her main job function was to investigate the viability of companies like Shepard Electronics and determine whether they were worth Wright's time and money to acquire. Most people assumed that the world of mergers and acquisitions was all about hostile takeovers, but a good portion of the deals were mutual and in Planks case much welcomed.

Obviously, he couldn't wait to shake himself of his burgeoning electronic firm. His eagerness wouldn't normally be a red flag. Some people were honest enough with themselves to know when they'd taken their companies as far as their abilities and assets allowed. Yet from their first meeting Jessica knew Planks was far from humble. No—his eagerness to be acquired by Wright Inc. had little to do with humility and everything to do with greed and like most men of his ilk, he assumed that no one would figure out his schemes.

"I hope you've found everything you need."

He said the words in dismissive nonchalance fueling her excitement.

She smoothed her thumb along the file folder in her hand. It contained a copy of her final report, detailing the viability of Planks' company and whether or not it represented a good investment.

This is going to be fun.

"Yes. Actually, I was able to complete my final analysis this afternoon. I sent it over to Mr. Wright before coming to see you," she said.

"Wonderful. I'll let my lawyers know to begin the paperwork so that we can move forward."

"That won't be necessary." She leaned forward and placed the file on the desk.

"Mr. Wright has elected to withdraw his bid for Shepard Electronics."

She watched as her words penetrated the thick fog of arrogance surrounding him. It didn't take long. His eyes widened for a brief moment before narrowing in anger while his smirking lips firmed into a grim line.

"What the hell are you talking about?"

He jacked forward in his chair and snatched the file open. His gaze blazing across the lines she'd enjoyed typing with relish.

Satisfaction skittered through her. Yes— moments like these were exactly why she loved her job. Some children grew up wanting to be doctors, firefighters or astronauts. She'd grown up wanting to make men like Planks wallow in their own failure.

A therapist might say her satisfaction stemmed from a childhood filled with disappointments caused by inattentive socialite parents, along with a dose of resentment at being abandoned. After authorities discovered their lavish lifestyle had been funded by a myriad of embezzlement and Ponzi schemes her parents fled the country in fear of imprisonment. Had they repented in any way? No. They merely chose a country with no extradition agreements with the United States and continued to live without care for their actions or daughter. Since Jessica was well aware of her motivations and baggage, she had no problem with forgoing potentially massive therapy bills for the lucrative six-figure salary she received by taking men like Planks down instead.

"I found the transfers. It took me a little while, but the thing about money is that it always leaves a trail. No business is squeaky clean, but those hefty deposits you've been moving into your accounts..."

She shook her head and pursed her lips—letting out a short tsking sound.

"Not a very smart move. So I'm sure you can understand why Mr. Wright wouldn't want to move forward with a company whose profit margins have been faked for the last six quarters," she said.

The crunching sound of paper rent the air as his fist clenched around the file. His knuckles paled into a glowing white; a stark contrast to the deep red flush racing up his neck to cover his scowling face in an angry mask.

"You fucking bitch!"

She raised an eyebrow at his snarled accusation.

Typical.

It never ceased to amaze her how easy some people found it necessary to resort to name-calling. On some level, she appreciated the last attempt at a jab. After all, in Planks' case she had just guaranteed that his family and colleagues would learn of his dirty dealings.

"Thank you," she said as she rose from her seat.

He leapt to his feet and leaned forward— bracing his hands down on the desk.

"You can't do this!"

Her gaze flicked down his body briefly before meeting his eyes dead on.

"I just did."

She turned on her heel and walked to the door—a string of expletives and curses raining down her back as she reached for the knob. She paused for a moment there.

"By the way. You might want to wipe the lipstick stains from your slacks before you go meet with your board of directors."

With that, she strode from the office, her only thoughts focused on seeing Lucas again.

* * *

RAPT

Available now via all major book retailers.

Turn the page for a sneak peek of the paranormal romance, **The Golden Pack Alphas** *by Laurel Cremant.*

Chapter One

Prey always made the same mistake—they ran.

Standing motionless at the floor-to-ceiling windows of his hotel room, Marcus Legrand looked out at the umbrella-dotted beach beyond. He savored the weight of anticipation and awareness that had cloaked him ever since he'd learned that Gigi had run—again.

A smile twitched his lips. She would never admit that, nor would she appreciate his use of the pet name he'd assigned to her. Strong-willed and stubborn, Georgia Walker never ran from anyone or anything—except him.

From the moment he'd first visited her pack, the prickly woman had loved to avoid and drive him crazy in equal measure.

As a High Council *Ma'at*, an enforcer of the laws and rites agreed upon hundreds of years ago by the original wolf packs, he preferred his life well-ordered. He knew all too well the chaos and destruction that came with flaunting pack rules.

He was that chaos. *He* was that destruction.

Gigi didn't seem to care. She was out there on the beach. No doubt celebrating her supposed coup in evading him.

It always amused him how easily a person underestimated a *were*—specifically a werewolf, and specifically *him*. But Gigi should have known better. As the daughter of Darius, the Golden Pack Alpha, she was more than privy to Council politics and the foolishness in taunting him. And yet, she did it anyway.

Her willingness to pick a fight stirred more than just the wolf in him—it woke the man. It had been a long time since any woman, shifter or otherwise, had aroused any interest in him. Even longer since one did more than make his cock twitch in interest. But from the moment he'd seen her and inhaled her heady scent, he'd wanted nothing else than to throw her over his shoulder and steal her away.

He'd been overwhelmed with that urge, and even now, after a year to come to terms with what it all meant, he struggled to tamp down on the compulsion to drag her to the nearest surface and fuck her until they both passed out into oblivion.

I have to catch her first.

Marcus gave a mental shrug. For him, the hunt was always the easy part. He reached up and ran his left hand along his opposite arm. Although covered by the thin layer of his shirt, he traced the fine lines of the tattoos beneath, every one as firmly etched into his memory as on his skin. Each symbolizing a kill or judgment made. Reminders of what he was, and the role he'd chosen to play.

Him being a lone wolf, the Council had recruited him years ago—more years than most knew. They'd taken him in, shielded his true origins, and in return, he'd become their hammer. The one they called upon to mete out justice. He'd never regretted his choice.

He understood the necessity of having a feared weapon on your side when approaching the bargaining table. Fear often created the best compromise. When the Council called upon his services, it signaled the end of negotiations.

He'd become accustomed to people watching

him with unease and deference. Even the few women he engaged with were more interested in the thrill of sleeping with an enforcer than anything else. Yet, Georgia's eyes contained a different look entirely.

Her deep brown gaze challenged and aroused with each glance, each raise of the brow, and each drop of eyelashes.

Thinking back on the cool reception she'd given him when he'd first arrived in Golden Valley a year ago, the sadistic part of him smiled at his choice of conquest. Unlike other women, Gigi was not in awe of him. She didn't hold her tongue or pretend meekness. Her countenance screamed Alpha, and had his wolf—and another part of his anatomy—standing up to take notice from the start.

She'd stood at her father's side, tall and proud, her long dark hair falling around her shoulders in waves, framing toffee skin and high, rounded cheekbones. Her plush mouth had firmed in disdain and she'd quirked one delicate eyebrow at him.

"Oh, goodie. The new pit bull is here."

Her husky voice had delivered the cutting words without a single waver or pause. He'd noted it as possibly the sexiest thing he'd ever heard.

At first, he'd believed his reaction stemmed from her heat cycle. He could smell it on her—the thick musk of her arousal swirling through his senses, almost drowning him in the need to slant her stubborn chin up and sink his teeth into the succulent flesh of her neck.

Despite her obvious initial dislike of him, her eyes had flared with an answering blaze of attraction.

Meeting her had tilted his whole world off its axis, and things would never be the same for him.

Whether she deigned to admit it, they'd both chosen at that moment to withdraw to their respective corners. He'd come to the valley on official orders from the Council and had no time for small dalliances or otherwise. Whatever reasons she had for retreating remained her own.

He'd been sent to help deal with a rogue pack. Gigi's father, not wanting to endanger his own people, had called upon the Council to help settle the matter. Rogue wolves proved dangerous on several levels. Not only did they refuse to obey the rules set in place to protect *weres* from discovery, they also had no respect for life, human or otherwise.

Under normal circumstances, the Council

would not have stepped in. Most rogue packs died a natural death. The absence of no true Alpha in the group always led to them killing each other off in a useless quest to dominate.

But this pack had been different. On top of deliberately breaking the rules, they'd begun kidnapping humans and turning them. That, the Council could not ignore.

Dealing with them hadn't taken much time. But there had been some casualties, one of them being Darius' Beta. In the end, the group had been defeated and dispatched, justice met, and his job done—seven new feathers added to his collection. However, during his stay, he'd developed an attachment to the Golden Pack that had been...unexpected.

After delivering his report to the Council, Marcus had returned to Golden Valley—and to Gigi.

As an enforcer, he had the right to set up base wherever he chose, and for the time being, he'd settled on the biting cold mountains of Golden Valley. He'd even agreed to play temporary Beta to Darius.

He liked the pushy Alpha. His twinkling eyes, booming voice, and ready smile could too easily be misconstrued as trusting and easy-going, but Marcus had seen him in battle. Darius proved to be one of the shrewdest wolves he'd ever encountered—and deadliest. Traits he had no doubt passed down to his only daughter.

The dynamic between Darius and the other wolves intrigued him.

None in the group resented their Alpha's choice in mate, Genevieve, Gigi's mother. Her being a witch didn't seem to bother the other wolves. Yet, for some, he'd seen that an obvious weariness of Gigi herself existed.

Her hybrid status put them on edge. A part of them questioned her right to belong. In that, he could sympathize with her. He understood the difficulties of being different in a world that expected sameness.

It felt strange to him—being surrounded by a collective. The feeling wasn't entirely bad. Just different.

He'd never given any consideration to becoming part of any one pack. Both his history and need for privacy didn't lend themselves to community living.

Yet, he'd stayed. He'd set up house in a small bungalow close to Darius' large home. He'd chosen the location in small part to be available

to Darius and in larger part to be near Gigi—
her cottage being only a few yards on the
other side of the main house. Each day, he
grew more attached to the land, and each day,
he wanted Gigi with a need that bordered on
obsession.

She avoided him, evaded his presence with
a skill he had to admire. He reveled in their
power struggle.

Just before her recent disappearing act,
he'd found her leaving her father's office, back
straight and eyes flashing.

"Bad day?"

"Fuck off."

"Such a lady."

"And you're such a pest."

*He reached out and touched her arm,
pausing her marching progression.*

"In a suicidal mood today?" she asked.

*"With you? Always. Now tell me what has
you so upset."*

*Her nostrils flared and she leaned into
him.*

*"You. You bother me. When are you going
to saddle up and find yourself a new pack to
annoy?"*

"Maybe as soon as you stop running."

Her lips curled up in a sneer.

"I don't run from anyone, Legrand. If I choose to not be around you, it means that I see no need in spending time with arrogant pricks."

He stroked a hand up her waist and brushed a fingertip over one tight nipple.

"And yet, those sensitive nipples of yours say differently every time I see you."

She returned the favor, running a hand down his front and cupped his hard cock.

"And your dick seems to have the same problem," she said, her voice almost sickly sweet.

Their gazes held as he pinched her nipple, and she squeezed his shaft.

"It would be a shame for you if I had to rip it off," she whispered before wrenching away from his hold and storming away.

He'd watched her walk away with a smile on his face. Even the threat of dismemberment hadn't been enough for his arousal to subside. He considered each encounter with her as progress. Soon, she would admit that there was more between them than just simple attraction.

Focusing back on the beach, he narrowed his gaze onto a specific pink umbrella poised haphazardly in the sand.

He touched a hand to his suit pocket, feeling the note folded inside. Darius had requested that he bring Gigi home for Christmas. But even if Darius hadn't asked him to find Gigi, Marcus would have come for her. They'd spent the last year tiptoeing around each other, and it had to stop.

Dropping his hands down to his sides, he turned from the window and strode to the door. Time to go hunting.

Chapter Two

Sunshine, rum punch, and hot men.

Hell, yeah.

Georgia Walker smiled—a contented sigh drifting across her lips as she adjusted the thin straps of her red and white bikini top. Nothing could compare to celebrating Christmas in the Caribbean.

No concerns over urgent emails, emergency meetings, or irate clients—and most importantly, she didn't have to worry about the pressure of being a pack Alpha's daughter or combat the suspicious looks of those who didn't trust her hybrid birth.

Being born to both a witch and a *were* came with certain privileges and drawbacks.

On one hand, she had the strength and stamina of a wolf; on the other, her ability to sense when others lied made more than one pack member wary. The fact that the usual dose of instinct and intuition shifters were normally gifted with became intensified by her mother's shaman heritage only seemed to make matters worse.

Not to mention her parents' recent penchant for matchmaking. She shuddered at the thought of being paraded around a room full of want-to-be Alphas. Lately, she could practically see thought bubbles of grandchildren floating around her mom's head.

So given a choice, she much preferred her current location rather than the week of holiday social events her mother planned every year with military precision.

About a two hours' drive east of Vancouver, her hometown, Golden Valley, sat nestled between tall, rolling mountains and crisp, dense green forests. She would always consider it home, but she had to admit that her current view on the beach held more than a little appeal.

Reclining back on her lounge chair, she closed her eyes and let the warmth of the sun sink into her bones.

The limb-freezing climate of British Columbia in winter had nothing on the powder-soft sandy beaches, warm, clear-blue waters, and cool breezes of Jost Van

Dyke.

She'd discovered the little island paradise a year ago while on a case and had never been so happy to stake out a cheating husband.

Her business, a private security and detective firm, had grown a lot in the last five years, and she rarely went on cases herself anymore, but she'd made an exception for her best friend, Kara. Georgia didn't make friends easily—a byproduct of spending most of her days either focused on building up her company or on pack politics. But when she'd hired Kara several years ago as an Internet security specialist, the quirky human had wormed her way into Georgia's heart.

When Kara had confided to her that she suspected her husband of cheating, Georgia had handled the investigation personally.

Although she'd returned home to deliver divorce-inducing news, she had done so with sun-streaked hair and a deeper tint to her brown skin.

Now, thanks to a few new lucrative contracts, she'd had no qualms in splurging on a last-minute vacation.

She looked forward to a few days without worrying about urgent emails, pack politics, and being away from *him*.

Marcus Legrand.

From the moment he'd stepped foot in Golden Valley, the tight-backed enforcer had set off clanging alarm bells to the tune of Iron Maiden's *The Number of the Beast* in her mind.

She reacted to him in a way she was woman enough to admit scared her almost witless.

Her usual abilities of intuition rang silent when it came to him. As if he'd constructed a lead wall around his mind and she couldn't get a read on him—ever.

She couldn't even anticipate his approaches, and he seemed to revel in his ability to sneak up on her.

But when he was near—her body went on high alert, as if it had been starved for him, and she didn't like it one bit.

When he'd first arrived a year ago, she'd been about to start her heat cycle and meeting him had hurtled her body head first into estrous.

Marcus embodied everything she'd fought against her entire life—loss of control.

From a young age, she'd always strived for discipline over the urges her wolf and

176

animal nature pushed on her. It was no secret that she was quick to temper, but few ever provoked her to the point of violence. Thanks to her quick wit and gift of clairvoyance, the use of intimidation and fear became her weapons of choice.

Her choice in path had more to do with self-preservation than any lofty ideas on violence.

She'd known early on that her wolf was strong, stronger than even her parents suspected. But a faction of wolves within the community were already suspicious of her. If they learned how much power she truly had, she would never be able to win them over.

The pack was all the family she had. Her mother had been an only child, and the coven she'd once belonged to had shunned her when she chose to mate with Georgia's father.

But all that didn't matter. Given a choice, she would always choose her pack.

Georgia had grown up in pack life and her wolf craved a sense of community. She would do anything to maintain that connection.

For that reason, she rarely shifted and would seldom be found during the group runs and hunts the pack engaged in. Remaining in her human form allowed her to avoid detection. Contrary to human myths and legends, werewolves weren't compelled to shift during full moon phases. The ability could be controlled except for the rare exceptions of *weres* with mental illnesses and instabilities.

She recalled the last time she'd shifted— during the rogue attacks the year before. Not only had it been the first time she'd shifted in months, it had also been the first time she'd seen Marcus' wolf.

Her father had assembled a small group of fighters, their goal not to engage the rogues but only to surround their camp while Marcus investigated. They'd gathered just outside of the forest surrounding Golden Valley, eager to route the unwanted wolves from their home territory.

Turning her back, she'd allowed her body contort slowly, making sure not to let her power flare. The others had shifted around her and she'd expected to feel the excitement that always occurred when her wolf recognized the chance to be free—at least for a moment. But this time, a burst of elation had burst through her heart so strong it had left her frozen in shock.

Her wolf had blazed a myriad of thoughts and images through her mind, but only one word had come through crystal clear.

Mate.

She'd leapt around, her gaze drawn to only one wolf—Marcus.

Her heart thrummed fast as she recalled the image of his wolf. He'd been beautiful. In that moment, she'd seen why the Council had chosen him as enforcer.

Large and hulking, his wolf almost resembled a bear. Even his fur was intimidating, spiked brown with blond tips, reminding her of sharpened spikes.

Shaking her head clear, she came back to the present.

Marcus was lethal in more than just his skills as an enforcer.

She refused to let her destiny be determined by a chemical impulse to mate, and his presence threatened the hard-won control she'd spent years honing.

The unfairness of it all galled her. The decision of who she spent the rest of her life with should be made by *her*. Not her overzealous wolf, and definitely not some hormonal urge.

Each day, her irritation grew as it became more difficult not to succumb to the urge of crawling onto the man's lap and sating the unending hunger that had been building since they'd first met.

All of that didn't matter now. For the next several days, she would be free from the worries that plagued her at home.

Taking a deep breath, she reached her arms overhead, arched her back, and inhaled the balmy salted air.

She could almost hear her muscles sigh, but despite the relaxation attempting to spread through her limbs, her body tingled with a tension settled too deep.

Her heat cycle was starting—nothing she could do to relieve the discomfort.

Well, almost nothing.

Dropping her hands back down to her sides, she swept her gaze across the small beach. It wasn't crowded but had a fair number of sunbathers and Zen cravers. And most importantly, it had men looking for the same thing she was—a little fun, forgetfulness, and zero strings.

Although heat pooled to her center, her stomach rolled in apprehension.

In the past, she'd had no problems finding a willing male to sleep with when she was in heat. She enjoyed sex, and although each year, her parents hoped she would choose a permanent mate, no man in or outside of her pack inspired much feeling or devotion. At least, not enough for her to be shackled to for life.

But since last year, because of *The-Wolf-Who-Shall-Not-Be-Named*, no one appealed to her.

Instead of rolling around for several hours with a well-endowed chosen playmate, she'd remained locked in her home for days with her vibrator and a healthy supply of batteries.

She had no intentions of repeating the experience. This week, she planned on proving to both her body and wolf that Marcus wasn't the only man capable of making her hot.

Her gaze combed the area, looking for a good candidate.

One particular man caught her eye.

He'd been swimming for the last hour, his caramel arms cutting through the water in languid strokes. But now, he rose out of the surf resembling a naughty sea nymph, his strong legs leading up to deep blue board shorts. Dry, she guessed the swimming trunks were perfectly modest—but wet, they molded to his thick, muscled thighs and cupped his cock in a way that left very little to the imagination. And since Georgia's imagination was better than the average wolf's, she bit back a groan and clenched her thighs tight.

Yum.

Pushing her sunglasses up to her hair, she licked her lips as her gaze traced the diamond-bright droplets of water running along his hard chest. They sluiced down his body, aided by the tight ridges of muscles along his abdomen, tunneling down to what looked like one hell of a stocking stuffer.

Merry Christmas to me.

Yes, an island getaway was proving to be the perfect holiday treat.

Her gaze meandered back up his chest and after taking a brief note of thick smooth lips and tempting dimples, she made eye contact with her merman come to life.

His eyes gleamed with interest and her lips turned up in her best come-hither smile. He took a step forward and then froze, his gaze focusing on something just over her left shoulder. Shaking his head, he turned and continued walking down the beach.

What the hell!

She frowned at his retreating back. Admittedly, she was no supermodel, but she'd never had a problem with luring men her way.

A long shadow fell over her.

Her turn to freeze. Despite him blocking out the sun, a heated scorch rippled down her torso and limbs as the approaching shade crept down her body. Her nipples pebbled to thick points, her pussy clenched, and a slow growl worked its way up her throat.

Only one thing made her body react this way, and she'd deliberately left it back in Golden Valley.

"Hello, Gigi. Miss me?"

* * *

THE GOLDEN PACK ALPHAS
Available now via all major book retailers.

Other Books by Laurel Cremant

Laurel Cremant
Romance Author

Laurel is a romance author, who like most writers loves to read. Her first love (pun intended) has always been romance. From the sappy YA romance novel to the more risqué erotica novels, Laurel is a sucker for a good love story.

After spending years working in science and data, in 2011 Laurel decided to finally put her love of romance and the written word to good use. With a love for romantic tension and snarky heroines, she penned her first romance novel and hasn't looked back.

Laurel writes paranormal and contemporary romance and is a self-proclaimed, out of the closet nerd. She admits that she can't seem to avoid adding a bit of "nerdology" or "geek-dom" to all of her books. Living in Miami, she also admits that she can't seem to avoid giving her heroines gorgeous shoes, "In Miami, we worship everything strappy, open toed and just plain hot!"

www.LaurelCremant.com

www.ingramcontent.com/pod-product-compliance
Lightning Source LLC
Chambersburg PA
CBHW021041130626
46552CB00005B/1954